WHO'S AFRAID OF THE BIG BAD WOLF?

Wolf Creek Pack 6

Stormy Glenn

MENAGE AMOUR

Siren Publishing, Inc.
www.SirenPublishing.com

A SIREN PUBLISHING BOOK
IMPRINT: Ménage Amour

WHO'S AFRAID OF THE BIG BAD WOLF?
Copyright © 2010 by Stormy Glenn

ISBN-10: 1-60601-380-7
ISBN-13: 978-1-60601-380-9

First Printing: September 2010

Cover design by Jinger Heaston
All cover art and logo copyright © 2010 by Siren Publishing, Inc.

Printed in the U.S.A.

PUBLISHER
Siren Publishing, Inc.
www.SirenPublishing.com

DEDICATION

To my love. My life wouldn't be complete without you. You saved me from a life of misery and gave me the world. There will never be words even I could write to say how much I love you.

WHO'S AFRAID OF THE BIG BAD WOLF?

Wolf Creek Pack 6

STORMY GLENN
Copyright © 2010

Chapter 1

Benjamin Nobles watched the procession of colorfully dressed men and women parade around the sacred circle from his nearly hidden view on the edge of the tree line. He grimaced as he stared at them twisting and turning before the throng of men and women hoping to find their mate.

Ben would have gladly given his right arm to be anywhere else but here. He did not like big gatherings such as this, but his alpha ordered him here. And he never disobeyed an order from his alpha—no matter how uncomfortable it made him feel. And this was about as uncomfortable as he could ever remember being.

The alpha, Daniel Nash, commanded that anyone unmated and of marriageable age to gather in the sacred circle of their pack to see all the men and women of mating age from Prince Zacarius's coven. And hopefully, a mating would take place. Just not for Ben.

Ben knew there would never be a mate for him. No one in his or her right mind would want to be shackled with a man such as him, a man with no tenderness, no gentleness, and, certainly, no kindness. He didn't even know what those emotions were anymore. They had been stripped from him, along with a good portion of his sanity.

Sometimes he even wondered if he had any humanity left in him. He was a monster, in body as well as in mind. His huge frame was filled compactly with bulging muscles, long strong legs that were as big as tree trunks, and arms the size of smaller tree trunks. Battle scars littered his body—including his face, with one long scar that curved from the corner of his right eye, down his cheek, to the bottom of his jaw.

He wouldn't be winning any beauty contest anytime soon. It was all most people could do just to look him in the eye without flinching. He had nothing to offer a mate and he knew it.

* * * *

Stefan stood there, his head slightly bent, his long hair falling forward, concealing his face from the large crowd he stood in. He had been ordered here by Prince Zacarius to stand before all of the unmated werewolves of Wolf Creek Pack so that they might find their mate. Stefan knew he was here for another purpose.

His stepbrother, Oliver, had made it very clear to Stefan last night as to why he stood here. Tonight he would be mated to Dane, a friend and cohort of Oliver's.

Oliver and Dane had done everything in their power over the last few months to persuade Stefan to agree to be mated to Dane. When that didn't work, the gloves came off and the real pain began. Dane wasn't Stefan's fated mate, but Oliver had decreed they would be mated anyway.

Under normal circumstances, Stefan would have been excited to be mated, anything to get away from his stepbrother. The previous night, Dane proved he was just as demented as Stefan's stepbrother when he slapped Stefan around, all while regaling Stefan with the things he planned to do once Stefan belonged to him.

Stefan guessed he had one thing to be thankful for where his stepbrother was concerned. Oliver made sure that Dane had never forced Stefan before now. He seemed to enjoy hanging the *mating* with Dane over his head.

Ever since their older brother, Desmond, lost his life trying to kill Prince Zacarius, Oliver had taken over as head of their family. At first, Stefan thought it wouldn't be so bad. He thought Oliver had to be better than his asshole brother, Desmond. Now he wasn't so sure.

Little by little, Oliver cut off Stefan's contact with the outside world. Stefan wasn't allowed to go anywhere or see anyone except Dane and Audley, Stefan's best friend and Dane's younger brother. Audley also had the distinction of being the man Oliver wanted to trade Stefan for.

Stefan fought Oliver's plan as much as he could. He refused to acknowledge Dane's orders, gaining himself more than a few bruises along the way but he refused to give in to their terror tactics.

With the orders from their prince, Stefan knew that his time was finally up. Dane would have him tonight. And there wasn't anything Stefan could do to stop it. His shoulders dropped as he began to give in to the despair filling his heart. For a brief moment, he let his gaze sweep over the room in the hopes that someone—anyone—would come save him.

* * * *

A small movement of ragged brown fabric to one side of the circle caught Ben's attention. He watched from the edge of the trees, his eyes never leaving the figure in brown. He caught sight of a small pale face glancing out from behind stringy hair.

The dirty strawberry-blond hair was not what caught Ben's attention. Nor was the length, which seemed to go on forever, from the top of the young man's head to just below the soft curve of his ass.

It was the huge sky-blue eyes that peeked out between the thick strands of hair. They were the most expressive eyes Ben had ever seen. Then the little man smiled at him, and Ben felt a strange tightening in the middle of his chest.

The world around him simply disappeared. It was only the young man and him. No one else existed. But as quickly as it had come, the smile disappeared, along with the beautiful eyes that had seemed to see into his very soul.

Ben leaned up on his feet to get a better look at him. At six-foot-nine, he stood taller than most men. In fact, he had never met anyone who was taller than him. There was nearly nothing that could make Ben leave the safety at the edge of the party. But the body was huddled down behind the horde of partygoers, and Ben couldn't get a good look. He felt a need to find the young man.

If he had been truly thinking about it, he would have questioned this obsessive need to find the man hiding on the other side of the circle. And then he would have run for his life. But all he could feel was an unnatural desire to hunt down the brown fabric and meet the man who smiled at him.

Ben left his safety at the edge of the trees and began working his way through the crowd, his eyes never leaving the young man. He knew the man could see him walking to him by the slight turning of his body toward him. He seemed to be waiting for Ben. From the small smile on his lips, Ben assumed the man would be happy to see him.

As he got closer to him, Ben could see more of his stature. He was small. He might reach Ben's sternum…if he stood on a stool. Otherwise, he would barely reach Ben's chest. The man couldn't have been more than five-foot-ten or so. His thread-worn outfit was definitely not made to look pleasing on him. There seemed to be no contours or soft places on him. On a whole, the clothing seemed to hang over him more like a sack than a shirt. It was not made to entice anyone, which was strange considering that's what tonight's gathering was all about.

The smile fell from the man's lips as Ben drew nearer to him, fear began to form in his deep blue eyes. Ben slowed his quick stride. He felt sorrow in his heart as he realized that the little man was afraid of him. Ben stopped a mere foot from him. He wanted to give the man the opportunity to flee from his side before he said anything to him.

As he tried to form the words that might keep the stunning man where he could look at him, Ben noticed that the man's gaze was not on him but on some unseen person behind him. He slowly turned as he felt a cold shiver creep up his spine.

A man walked slowly toward them, a look of triumph plastered on his thin lips. He was a vampire. Ben could tell even from here. He looked back down at the young man. His fear was almost tangible. Before his eyes, the man began to shake.

It came suddenly to Ben that the little man wasn't afraid of him. He was afraid of the vampire walking toward them. He wasn't even looking at Ben. His entire being was centered on the man coming toward them, and his body was readying itself to flee.

"Dane," the little man whispered, terror lacing his thin voice.

Ben wondered if an eternity from know he would understand why he did what he did, but for now, it was a complete mystery to him. He only knew that he had to get the young man to safety, to protect him. Reaching out, he grabbed his arm and began dragging him through the crowd. The man gasped as he was pulled along.

Ben stopped suddenly when the smarmy-looking man stepped in front of him. He felt the smaller man plow into his back and reached around behind him to place a steadying hand on him.

"Are you claiming Stefan?" Dane asked.

Ben suddenly realized what he was doing. His only thought was to save Stefan, not to claim him. His stomach rolled just by the thought of it. He couldn't have a mate. "Why do you ask?" Ben growled.

"Because if you do not claim him, I will," Dane said as he stepped around Ben and reached for Stefan. "Stefan, come," he stated triumphantly.

Ben could feel the terror filling Stefan by the shaking in his body. "You will not!" he snarled as he stepped between them. He didn't know why, but he knew he could not let this man take Stefan from him. "He is not your mate."

"If you do not claim him, then he is fair game for the rest of us," he said as he reached for Stefan again, grabbing his wrist. Stefan seemed to make his body as small as possible as he pressed up against Ben.

"Touch him and die!" Ben snarled as he pulled Stefan from the man's grasp, wrapping an arm around Stefan's waist and pulling him back against his larger body.

"Ben," said a strong voice behind him "What goes on here?"

Ben turned toward the voice, knowing it was his alpha. "Nothing goes on here, Daniel."

The man beside him sputtered, "That's not true, Alpha Nash. This man is refusing my claim on Stefan."

Alpha Daniel Nash looked over at the arm that Ben had wrapped around the waist of the cowering man. "Ben, if you do not claim this man, then you must give him up to he who will."

Ben's body went stiff at his alpha's words. He didn't want to claim Stefan. He always believed that he would spend his life alone. Then he heard a small whimper come from the frightened man pressed against him. He knew his choices were gone.

"Then I claim him."

Daniel looked down at the bent head of the shaking man. "Are you sure, Ben?"

"I claim him!" Ben growled as he lifted his wrist and bit into it.

Once he felt the blood start to flow down his wrist, he held it to the small man's mouth, forcing him to drink. At the same time, he leaned down and sank his canines into the soft flesh between Stefan's neck and shoulder.

He heard a small whimper come from Stefan before the elation of the man's sweet blood swept through him, before he was forced to close his eyes to hide the ecstasy and desire that instantly filled his body.

The wolf in him demanded that he take his mate's body as well as his blood. The man in him tried desperately to regain the control that was rapidly draining from him. Stefan's blood was unlike anything Ben had ever tasted. It was like sunshine and earth all rolled into one, with a side of lust thrown in for good measure. Ben was entranced.

He started to lift the small man up to claim that which was now his by divine right when he heard a small cry fall from Stefan's lips. Then he tasted his fear. It was the only thing he knew would have gotten through to him in his aroused state.

Licking the small wound he had been drinking from, Ben lifted his head and gazed back into wide sky-blue eyes. Stefan stared at him like he had never seen a claiming before. And maybe he hadn't seen one quite like this. It had been rough and animalistic, much like him.

Ben shrugged his shoulders. He might as well go on as he was now. He didn't plan on changing for this small man any more than he had to. If anything, Stefan would be accommodating to him. He was a werewolf warrior, one of the alpha's chosen soldiers. Warriors did not change for anyone but their alpha.

Ben looked down into the frightened man's eyes. "Close it," he demanded, indicating his bleeding wrist. Stefan leaned his head back and stared up at him, his lips still wrapped around the wound.

"Close it, Stefan," he whispered again, this time only for his ears. Ben shuddered as Stefan's tongue swept across the ripped flesh at his wrist.

Ben watched as Stefan's eyes quickly darted up to his, then down again as his tongue made another quick swipe over his wrist, almost as if Stefan loathed giving up the potent taste of his bleeding flesh.

Ben looked down at Stefan's head for several moments before wrapping his arm around the man's waist again and looking at his alpha. "Thus, Stefan is claimed," he stated simply, even as he grabbed

Stefan's arm and pulled him behind him, walking through the crowd toward the edge of the sacred circle.

While most of his mind was on escaping from the masses gathered, he did hear the tittering of voices raised in anger begin between his alpha and the man who thought to claim Stefan as his own. A wicked smile briefly graced his lips as he heard the angry voice of his alpha put the man in his place.

"Enough! He has been rightfully claimed and now belongs to Ben."

Ben felt elation unlike any he had ever felt in battle flow through him at that statement. Stefan now belonged to him.

* * * *

Stefan was more confused than he had ever been in his life. As he fell into step beside the tall man who just claimed him, Stefan tried to gather his thoughts into some semblance of order. So much had happened in just a few moments.

He had seen the tall man from across the circle. He had looked so out of place, so uncomfortable that he felt the need to give him a small smile. Stefan's mother always said that a smile went a long ways toward making someone feel better. And he seemed like someone who needed to feel better. Stefan had no idea what a can of worms that would open for him.

From the moment he arrived, he knew Dane would claim him. His brother and Dane had both told him to just wait for Dane to claim him and do nothing else to draw attention to himself. Somehow, Stefan thought that he had not achieved that goal. There had been a lot of attention centered on him. And Dane had not claimed him.

Dane had not claimed him! Stefan felt a tremor of exhilaration flow through his body as he realized that Dane had not claimed him. Dane could never claim him now. Not only had someone else claimed him, he had been claimed by a member of a wolf pack. He was free of Dane and his stepbrother forever.

Just as suddenly, the feeling of joy fled from him to be replaced with confusion. Stefan stumbled as he realized that he might not belong to Dane, but he now belonged to one of the Wolf Creek Pack's biggest and most feared warriors.

Even hidden away on his father's estate as he had been for the last few months, Stefan had heard of Benjamin Nobles, Wolf Creek Pack's most fierce soldier. The man was practically a legend among werewolves and vampires alike.

He knew anyone in their right mind would be terrified of the big man, but Stefan wasn't. He was captivated by him. Ben seemed big and strong, yet Stefan saw something in the man's golden eyes that made him seem vulnerable at the same time. Stefan wanted to cradle the large man to him and take away all of his worries.

Then he wanted to take away all of his clothes. Stefan couldn't believe how aroused he was by the simple way the man smelled—all woodsy and male like. It made Stefan's legs quake but not with fear. Stefan's friend, Devlin, told him it would be like this when he met his mate. Stefan just didn't believe him at the time. He was wrong.

Ben suddenly stopped. Stefan barely contained his small cry of surprise when the man simply picked him up and cradled him in his massive arms. His touch was strong but gentle as he began walking again.

Stefan's rigid body began to slowly relax against Ben's. When Ben first picked him up, he had been terrified that the man would punish him for foolishly not obeying his words to seal the mating bite. But Ben seemed to have forgotten that little act of defiance. Instead, he seemed bent on getting away from the crowd and to someplace quiet.

Stefan settled down into Ben's arms, his head coming to rest on his wide chest. He allowed a brief smile to touch his lips as he realized that his new mate was much bigger than either Dane or

Oliver. He could beat them both with his hands tied behind his back. Maybe this mating thing wasn't so bad.

Reaching his home, Ben opened the door and walked in, shutting and locking the door behind him before setting Stefan down on his feet. He let his hand slide down Stefan's arm to his hand, grabbing it and pulling him along behind him as he walked through the house.

"This is my house," he stated sternly. "It's not much, but it's mine."

Stefan gazed around him as Ben led him from room to room. Ben had a nice house. It was much nicer than the small room he inhabited back where his brother lived. As he followed behind Ben, listening to him talk about each room, he nodded his head slowly.

He understood what Ben told him. This was Ben's house. Stefan might be here for a little while, but it would always be Ben's house, never Stefan's. It was a little disappointing, but nothing more than he expected.

Ben had no reason to share what was his with Stefan. And it wasn't like Stefan had anything to share with Ben. He had nothing of value. Over the last few months, Oliver had taken anything that might be worth something and sold it. Stefan basically had a few clothes and a couple of personal items.

Considering that Dane hadn't claimed him, Stefan wasn't even sure he had that. Oliver and Dane were going to be pissed that someone else had claimed him. Stefan didn't think they would be charitable enough to give him his meager belongings.

"This is where we sleep," Ben said as he came to his bedroom, catching Stefan by surprise.

Stefan looked around the large room, taking in the extra-large bed, the dresser, and two nightstands. It was a nice room, very clean looking. He liked this room. The bed looked very inviting, and, considering he had just been mated, Stefan was excited about trying it out.

"You can cook?"

Stefan looked up at Ben again, nodding his head. Ben wanted him to cook him something? Now?

"Good. I'm hungry. The kitchen's that way," Ben said, pointing over Stefan's head.

Stefan wanted to ask what he should cook, but thought better of it when Ben lifted an eyebrow at his hesitation. He quickly made his way to the kitchen and started looking through the cupboards to see what Ben had. He would need a lot to feed a man of Ben's size.

As he started pulling items from the refrigerator, he heard a noise behind him. His heart beat wildly in his chest as he spun around to find Ben sitting down at the table, watching him intently with a strange look in his eyes.

His hands trembled as he turned back around and finished gathering items and set them on the counter. He quickly broke several eggs into a bowl and started whipping them together.

He tried to keep his eyes off of Ben's gorgeous body and on the food he was preparing as he diced an onion, but every time he turned around, Ben was watching him. It was nerve-racking. Stefan didn't know what Ben wanted, and he couldn't help hoping that whatever it was, it involved the big bed in the other room.

As quickly as he could, Stefan cooked up a large omelet for Ben, sliding it onto a plate and setting it down on the table in front of him before crossing over to clean up the mess he had made.

"You not eating?"

Stefan turned to look at Ben in surprise before shrugging his shoulders. He wasn't sure how to answer Ben. He was hungry—very hungry—but Ben had said nothing about Stefan eating as well. He hadn't known he could.

He kind of got used to having to ask permission to eat over the last few months. Oliver always made him ask for food, if not outright beg. Until Ben claimed him, he hadn't had blood in what seemed like forever.

"I could eat," he whispered quietly, watching Ben as he waited for his reaction. Ben just bit into his omelet before gesturing with his fork for Stefan to make himself something. He sure wasn't one for words.

Not wanting to let the chance go by, Stefan quickly scrambled together two eggs, cleaning up his mess as he went. Sliding the eggs onto a plate, he cautiously walked to the table. His eyes watching for Ben's response, he sat down across from him and began eating.

"Do you need more blood?"

Stefan shrugged. "I'm okay for now." He wasn't, not really. He could use more blood, but he wasn't about to ask for it. He learned the hard way to not ask for what he wanted, to just be thankful for receiving what he needed.

"How often will you need to feed?" Ben asked casually, but Stefan could see that the idea bothered him by the tension in the man's shoulders. It seemed to bother just about anyone who wasn't a vampire. He'd have to remember that.

"I'm good for a couple of days."

Stefan knew he needed to feed more often than he had been. Eventually his strength would start to go, but asking a werewolf warrior to submit to feeding a vampire just didn't seem like the safest thing he could do. Stefan couldn't take blood from anyone else now that he was mated with Ben, but he'd have to be sure not to ask for too much, only when he was desperate.

As he finished his last bite and set his fork down on his plate, Stefan looked up to find Ben leaning forward in his chair, his elbows resting on the table, his chin on his clasped hands. His eyes were intently watching him again. He seemed to be trying to figure something out, but Stefan had no idea what.

Lowering his eyes, Stefan picked up his plate and reached for Ben's before getting to his feet and going to the sink. Quickly washing off the two plates and pans he had used, he set them in the dish rack, then turned back to Ben.

His eyes widened when Ben stood to his feet and held out his hand. "Come."

Stefan felt a bit of excitement as he took hold of Ben's hand, following him back to the bedroom. Was Ben going to claim him now? He was so wrapped up in his thoughts, he nearly jumped out of his skin when Ben reached behind him and closed the door.

"Go shower."

What?

Stefan's eyes flew up to look at Ben in shock, but he had already turned away, starting to pull his shirt off. Wondering why Ben wanted him to shower, but not stupid enough to argue with him, Stefan quickly went into the bathroom and began undressing.

He winced when the rough material of his shirt rubbed against the soft skin on his back as he pulled it up over his head. Tossing the shirt on the floor, he reached for his pants, quickly dropping them on top of his shirt.

The injuries he'd received from Dane's last visit to his brother's house marred his back and made him ache with every movement. As a vampire, Stefan knew he'd heal fast enough, but it was a real bitch in the meantime.

Stefan inhaled suddenly as he realized he would never be forced to *visit* with Dane again. He'd never feel the hard leather against his back as Dane tried to teach him his place. Stefan covered his mouth with his hand to silence his cry of joy. He was free.

Climbing into the shower with a little bounce in his step, he turned on the water, just standing under it for several moments, feeling the water spray over his shoulders and down his body. Damn, that felt good. He could soak under the hot water for hours.

"Stefan?"

Or not. Stefan turned to look out the shower door to where Ben stood in the doorway, his gaze on the floor. "Yes?" he answered quietly.

"Hurry up. It's time for bed," Ben replied before turning away.

Stefan quickly shampooed his hair, then scrubbed down as much of his body as he could without hurting himself. Regretfully turning off the water, he opened the shower door and grabbed a towel, drying himself off.

As he reached for his clothes, he suddenly realized that they were gone. His eyes went to the door. Had Ben taken his clothes? What was he supposed to wear? A smile?

"Huh, Ben? My clothes—"

"Counter," Ben replied.

Stefan turned to see a large white shirt folded on the counter. Picking it up, he shook it out and held it up to his body. He started to giggle, quickly covering his mouth with his hand as his eyes darted toward the bathroom door.

The shirt went all of the way down past his knees. It had to be Ben's. Pulling it over his head, he wondered why Ben had given him a shirt to wear. If he was going to be claimed, wouldn't it be better done naked?

Stefan walked into the bedroom. Ben lay in the bed, the blankets pulled up to his waist. His arms were folded behind his head. Stefan wondered if Ben was indeed going to finish the claiming. He hoped so.

Walking to the edge of the bed, Stefan almost ducked when Ben flipped the blankets back and gestured for him to get in. His breath held tightly in his chest, Stefan crawled into the bed and lay down.

His eyes closed briefly at the pleasure of the soft pillows. They were so soft his head just seemed to melt right into them. Back at home, he didn't even have a pillow. This was heaven.

"Stefan, come," Ben said.

Stefan opened his eyes to see Ben gesturing for him to move closer. Stefan swallowed the lump in his throat as he looked at the arms Ben held open to him. As slowly as he could, he moved over to lie down next to Ben, his heart pounding wildly as Ben's arms wrapped around him.

As Ben pushed his head down onto his large chest, Stefan could feel his chest rumble as he spoke. "Sleep, Stefan."

Sleep? Did that mean Ben wasn't going to finish claiming him? Why not? They were mated. They had every right to be intimate. Didn't they? And the quicker they finished the claiming, the safer Stefan would be.

"Ben?" Stefan murmured quietly, tilting his head to look up at him.

"Sleep, Stefan," Ben repeated.

Crap! So much for being claimed. Stefan closed his eyes and snuggled down against Ben. He could feel all of his hard contours, the thick muscles of the arms that held him, the hard chest beneath his head. It all felt so wonderful.

Stefan cautiously moved his hand up to rest it on Ben's chest, not sure how he would react. He heard Ben inhale as he began making small circles in his chest hair with his fingers. Ben suddenly moved his hand up to lay it over the top of Stefan's, stopping his movements.

Stefan had to smile. Ben hadn't removed his hand from his chest, just stopped his movements. Stefan turned his hand over, grasping Ben's. He gave him a small squeeze, holding his breath as he waited for Ben's response, if any.

A moment later, Ben squeezed his hand back. "Go to sleep, Stefan."

Stefan closed his eyes, the smile still gracing his face as he faded off to sleep. There was always tomorrow.

Chapter 2

Stefan opened his eyes slowly. For a brief moment, he wondered where he was. Then, as the events of the previous night filled his head, he quickly turned, looking for Ben, only to find the other side of the bed empty. Where was Ben?

Sitting up, he looked around the room. It was deserted. Stefan threw the blankets back and crawled from the bed. He quickly went to the bathroom to see if Ben was there. Finding it vacant, he slowly walked through the rest of the house.

He walked into the kitchen and found Ben sitting at the table. He held a cup of coffee in one hand, a newspaper in the other. Stefan took a moment to just look at him. Ben truly was magnificent.

He was dressed in nothing but a pair of jeans, his chest and feet bare. The mere width of Ben's shoulders was stunning on its own. He looked like he could carry an entire house on his shoulders, not to mention the sheer size of his arms.

Stefan didn't know if he was a minority or not, but Ben's size was more arousing than anything he had ever encountered before. It made him feel safe and protected, something Stefan had never experienced before. He seemed to spend his life being afraid.

The sight of Ben's naked chest, smattered with dark chest hair, plain out turned Stefan on. He wanted to run his fingers through that hair and discover where the small trail going down the man's abdomen led to.

"Did you need something, Stefan?" Ben asked without turning his head.

Stefan could feel his face heat up as he walked toward Ben. Guess he had been caught. However, he wasn't embarrassed enough to stop looking. Or to not climb on to Ben's lap and try to get a feel of that glorious chest.

Devlin told him that he would be attracted to his mate, but Stefan had no idea he would feel obsessed like this. He couldn't stop looking, stop wanting to smell the man. If this was what being mated felt like, Stefan was all for it.

As Ben looked up at him in confusion, Stefan swung his leg over Ben's lap, straddling his legs, his hands coming to rest on Ben's wide chest. He rubbed his hands over Ben as he slowly raised his eyes to meet Ben's golden ones.

"Good morning." Stefan giggled at the sight of total shock on Ben's face. He felt pretty sure his usual shy demeanor hadn't prepared Ben for this. Stefan couldn't explain it beyond the fact that Ben was now his mate.

He wanted the man. Everything about Ben aroused Stefan to a fever pitch, from the top of his gorgeous dark head to the bottoms of his big feet. The man was truly breathtaking, and just knowing that Ben was his nearly made Stefan melt.

"Is there—did you need something, Stefan?" Ben asked again, his voice going low and deep, filled with apprehension as he gazed down at Stefan.

"I imagine there are lots of things I need, but there is only one thing I want," Stefan replied as he leaned up to press his lips against Ben's. As he tried to push his tongue past Ben's lips, he felt Ben's hands press against his shoulders, pushing him back. With a deep heavy sigh, Stefan leaned back and looked into Ben's eyes.

"Stefan? Do you know what you're doing?"

Stefan's lips curled into a small grin as he grabbed Ben's hands from his shoulders and moved them down to his ass. "Yep," he whispered just before he leaned up to kiss Ben again. He wanted his mate to claim him. Now!

Ben opened his mouth and kissed Stefan back. Stefan could feel Ben's large hands clench his ass through the thin material of his shirt. Never letting his lips leave Ben's, Stefan reached down with his hands and grabbed his shirt, pulling it up until Ben was holding bare flesh in his hands.

He could feel Ben's response in the tightening of the man's hands on his ass, the soft moan that came from Ben's lips as his tongue moved out to brush against Stefan's, and the hard throbbing of Ben's cock between his legs.

"Stefan," Ben growled as he ripped his lips from Stefan's. "Baby, you don't know what you're doing."

"I know exactly what I'm doing. I'm asking—no, I'm demanding that my mate claim me."

* * * *

Ben's eyebrows shot up in surprise at Stefan's words. "Stefan—" Ben began, only to be stopped by Stefan placing his finger against his lips.

He watched with astonishment as Stefan grabbed the edge of his shirt and pulled it up over his head, tossing it to the floor, baring his entire body to Ben's hungry gaze. "Fuck, Stefan!" he whispered in awe as his eyes traveled over him.

Stefan was beautiful. Compared to Ben, he was almost delicate. His neck was long and swan like. His hairless chest, as small as it was, was nicely contoured with rippling muscles. Even his gorgeous light-brown nipples looked dainty.

As Ben's eyes moved farther down Stefan's body, he realized that there was one thing on Stefan's body that was not delicate. His cock was perfect, a nicely-rounded head leading down to a thick-veined shaft. And it was right there, pointing up at him from Stefan's hairless groin.

"Oh, sweet hell," he whispered as Stefan leaned back against the table, giving him much more of a view of that beautiful cock. Ben's hand trembled as he brought it around Stefan's body and brushed his fingers gently against the drops of liquid pooling from the small slit on top.

His eyes flew up to Stefan's when the man groaned, only to find them closed, his head dropped back on his shoulders. Oh God, he looked breathtaking. Ben tried to stay away from Stefan—really he did—but Stefan made it impossible.

Wrapping his hands around Stefan's small waist, he lifted him up on the table. Before Stefan could even voice the protest forming on his lips, Ben leaned down and wrapped his lips around Stefan's hard cock, running his tongue across the top and licking up the droplets there.

He growled deeply as the taste of Stefan exploded on his tongue. He was sweet and tangy and just about perfect. He couldn't believe that not only did this little man belong to him, he was demanding to be claimed. And Ben was helpless to deny Stefan a moment longer.

Pressing his tongue along the small slit, Ben pressed his lips closer together and moved them up and down Stefan's length. He smiled around Stefan's cock as he felt his hands clench in his long hair, pulling him closer.

Ben wasn't sure that Stefan had any clue about the monster that he had unleashed with his demand. He wanted Stefan more than he could ever remember wanting anyone. He hungered for Stefan so much he could feel his cock throbbing in his jeans, begging for freedom.

Knowing he didn't have much longer, Ben lifted his head. A small smile crossed his lips at Stefan's groan of protest. *Just wait, baby*, he thought as he grabbed Stefan's ankles and placed them on the table next to his hips before pushing his knees apart.

When Stefan turned bright red, a small squeak escaping his mouth as he tried to close his legs, Ben raised his eyes to meet his. "You started this, baby. If you want it to stop, now is the time to say something."

Ben held his breath as Stefan gazed up at him for several moments before slowly letting his legs fall apart again. As he turned his eyes down to the bounty before him, Ben wasn't sure he would ever breathe again.

Placing his hands on Stefan's inner thighs, he slowly ran his thumbs down around the edge of his cock, then slowly over Stefan's silky sac. He watched with fascination as the small sac tightened, drawing up close to Stefan's body.

Rubbing one thumb gently over Stefan's balls, the other thumb moved down to lightly caress the small puckered hole below. As he watched Stefan quiver in response, he quickly brought his finger to his mouth, getting it wet before pressing it against him.

As he pushed his finger in, he realized that Stefan was so tight that it would take a lot to loosen him up enough to accommodate Ben's large size. He would have to be very careful not to hurt his little mate.

On the other hand, he also realized that Stefan's tightness meant he had never been breached before. Knowing that he would be the first to claim Stefan almost made Ben come in his jeans. He had to dig his fingernails into the palm of his hand just to distract himself.

He looked up quickly when Stefan began pushing back with his hips, pressing more of Ben's finger in as he cried out. He was mesmerized as he watched creamy-white liquid shoot out of the top of Stefan's cock, spraying his stomach.

Damn, that was hot!

Ben quickly scooped up some of the liquid, coating his fingers with it before pressing two fingers in, moving them around to stretch Stefan out. It just made Stefan cry out more, his head thrashing back and forth on the table.

"More," Stefan begged.

Ben was happy to oblige, pressing in a third finger. As he moved his fingers around, he knew he had brushed against the man's prostate when Stefan's cries started to rise, nearing shouting level.

Abruptly standing to his feet, he continued to push his fingers in and out of Stefan as his other hand reached to pull at the buttons of his jeans, pushing his pants down his legs. Pulling his fingers free, he grabbed his hard cock and pushed it against Stefan's quivering flesh.

As he slowly began to push into Stefan, he bent over his body, grabbing his face in his hands to hold his head still. As Stefan raised his eyes to his, he lowered his head and claimed his lips even as his body claimed him.

Ben could hear Stefan's quick inhale as he pushed in to the hilt. He held himself still, waiting for Stefan to become accustomed to his size. But his lips continued to plunder Stefan's, nipping and licking with his tongue.

When he felt Stefan begin to respond to him again, he reached down and grabbed Stefan's hips, slowly thrusting into him. The tight grip of Stefan's body around his aching cock took his breath away. It was exquisite. He never wanted it to stop.

Sadly, he knew it was about to. He could feel his balls drawing up close to his body. He knew he was just a few thrusts away from release, and he wanted Stefan to join him. He wanted Stefan to experience the same joyous pleasure he did.

With one hand, he grabbed Stefan's long strawberry-blond hair and tilted his head to one side. With the other, he reached down between them and grabbed Stefan's cock, quickly stroking him even as his thrusts became more ferocious.

Ben looked down into Stefan's unfocused sky-blue eyes for a moment, amazed at the desire shining in them. Stefan actually looked like he wanted this—wanted Ben—and not just because of their mating. It filled Ben with more joy than even the feeling of Stefan's body did.

"Stefan," he growled in desperation as he felt his orgasm explode over him. As he erupted inside of Stefan, filling him with his release, he sank his canines into the soft flesh of Stefan's neck, drinking in his life essence.

As the knot inside of his cock extended to take hold inside of Stefan, Ben heard the man cry out, filling the space between them and covering Ben's hand with his seed. He moved his hips a few more times, satisfaction filling him when Stefan cried out more.

He had never knotted anyone before. That was reserved for mates only. But he had heard about the effects from his friend, Joe. If he continued to move his hips while knotted inside of Stefan, it would only increase the man's pleasure. He knew Joe was correct when Stefan cried again.

Ben finally collapsed down on Stefan, holding the mass of his weight off of him by his arms as he lifted his head to look down at him. He chuckled at the dazed look in Stefan's eyes as he looked back.

"Wow!" Stefan whispered, his voice sounding raspy and uneven.

"Yeah, wow." Ben chuckled.

"Is it always like that?"

"I don't know. This is the first time someone ever demanded that I claim them."

Ben watched with a great deal of amusement as Stefan's face turned red, his eyes suddenly dropping away. He seemed to take several deep breaths before looking back up at him. The grin that started to cross Stefan's face made Ben very nervous.

"If being demanding means that I get more of you, then consider me bossy." Stefan giggled.

Stefan's joy was infectious. Ben couldn't help laughing right along with him. He stopped suddenly, the sound of his own laughter sounding foreign to him. He couldn't actually remember the last time he had been amused by anything.

"Ben?"

Ben wrapped his arms around Stefan and sat back in his chair. He couldn't contain his small moan as Stefan's body settled down on his. He could really get used to being inside of his little mate.

"Ben? Are you okay?" Stefan asked again.

"Yeah, baby. I'm just fine," Ben said as he brushed the long hair back from Stefan's face. His eyes gazed over Stefan's face to his long, strawberry-blond hair. "I'd really like to brush this out sometime, Stefan. Would you let me do that?"

Stefan giggled. "You can do anything to me that you want. I'm all yours."

Ben gave a little smile as he looked back at his face. "Anything? That opens up a whole lot of possibilities, Stefan."

"And I hope to try out every single one of them."

Ben raised a dark eyebrow at his statement. Stefan seemed to have no problem with the physical side of their relationship. While it made Ben feel like he could fly, he wondered if it would last when the reality of being mated to him really hit Stefan.

He was honest enough with himself to know that he didn't have much to offer Stefan. He spent the majority of his adult life fighting and protecting the Wolf Creek Pack. He knew how to be strong and powerful, to uphold the laws decreed by his alpha. He did not know how to be gentle and caring, things Stefan deserved.

"Stefan, why are you here?" Ben asked quietly as he looked down at him.

Stefan cocked his head to one side, confusion drawing a frown on his face. "I don't understand. You claimed me, Ben. I'm your mate. Where else would I be?"

Ben shook his head. "No, I mean, why are you here? You could have denied my claim. Why did you accept me?" he asked hesitantly, almost afraid of the answer. He watched with fascination as Stefan's face turned red again and he bowed his head. "Stefan?"

Stefan mumbled something as he buried his face in Ben's neck and wrapped his arms around his shoulders. Ben was suddenly worried when Stefan refused to lift his face out of his neck. What could Stefan have to say that would have him so embarrassed?

"Stefan? Tell me," he demanded softly as he rubbed his hands up and down Stefan's back, trying to reassure him.

"I like the way you smell," Stefan whispered into his ear after a moment.

Ben heard his words, but it took several moments for their meaning to filter through his foggy brain and make sense to him. When they finally did, he could feel his heart start beating faster. Of all of the things Stefan could have told him, he never expected that.

Stefan had allowed himself to be claimed because he liked the way that Ben smelled? Was it possible that his little mate might actually be attracted to him? Just the thought brought his cock back to life deep inside of Stefan.

He could hear Stefan's soft moan as he hardened inside of him, filling him to capacity. Ben's own moan soon followed when Stefan's inner muscles tightened around him. "Stefan," he whispered desperately as his hands moved down to grasp his hips. Stefan began moving his hips up and down, his arms still wrapped around Ben's wide shoulders.

* * * *

"Ben," Stefan moaned as he licked the side of Ben's neck, nibbling at the hard chords of muscles with his teeth. He could feel Ben's response in the tightening of his hands on his hips, the throbbing of Ben's cock inside of him. He wanted him so bad he could taste it.

When Ben suddenly stopped moving and pulled out of him, Stefan cried out his protest, only to yelp when Ben picked him up and turned him over, settling his body down over the table. Before he knew it, Ben was standing behind him, pushing back into him with one huge lunge.

Stefan cried out his delight as his hands grabbed at the edge of the table to hold himself in place as Ben pounded into him hard and fast. He wanted to pull his legs up, but he couldn't seem to gain any leverage. Ben thrust into him too furiously.

Even with Stefan holding on to the edge of the table, Ben was pushing him forward with every plunge, the entire table starting to move across the floor. If Stefan hadn't been so busy groaning, he would have laughed. His mate was very strong.

When the pressure of his legs hitting the side of the table became too much, Stefan reached back with his arm to touch Ben's hip. "Ben, wait."

He was pleased when Ben stopped moving instantly. No matter what anyone else thought, he knew that his mate was caring and gentle. Ben wouldn't do anything to hurt Stefan, even at his own personal costs.

Stefan quickly let go of the table and climbed onto it, his legs spread apart. Laying his head down flat against the hard oak surface, he reached back again and grabbed the edge of the table before smiling over his shoulder at Ben. "Okay."

As he closed his eyes, he heard Ben's deep growl as he began thrusting into him again. One of Ben's hands moved down to clutch his ass, moving around and caressing each muscled globe. The other hand reached up to grab Stefan's hair, winding the long strands around his fingers until he controlled the movement of Stefan's head.

Stefan suddenly felt Ben's quick breath on his cheek. Opening his eyes, he turned his head slightly to see Ben leaning over him, his lips pulled back over clenched teeth. The whites of Ben's eyes were nearly gone, giving them a deep golden-copper color.

"Do you like this, Stefan? Do you like my hard cock in your ass?" Ben growled into Stefan's ear.

Stefan nodded his head.

"I can't hear you, Stefan? Don't you like what I'm doing to you? Do you want me to stop?"

"No! No, don't stop. Please don't stop," Stefan begged desperately.

"Then answer me, my little mate. Do you like having my cock buried in your ass?" Ben asked before licking the soft skin between Stefan's neck and shoulder.

"YES!" Stefan screamed.

"Are you going to come for me, little man? Are you going to squeeze those wonderful muscles of yours around my cock and make me come until I fill this sweet ass of yours? Until I knot inside of you?" Ben growled.

Stefan couldn't believe how erotic it was to hear Ben talking dirty to him, demanding his response. He never envisioned that he would be so aroused by dirty talk, but it was driving him out of his mind. The pulsing in his cock told him he was mere moments away from doing exactly what Ben wanted.

"Ben, bite me!" Stefan demanded as he wrapped one arm around Ben's neck and pulled his face down into the crook of his neck. "Claim me."

As he felt Ben's teeth immediately sink into his neck, he let go of the edge of the table to reach between his legs and grab his cock, stroking it several times before he cried out. His release shot from him and covered the table and the floor beneath.

His breathing erratic, he could hear Ben's deep growl in his ear as he licked his bite closed. "Ben, I need—" Stefan wasn't quite sure what it was that he needed. He just knew he needed something from Ben.

Stefan thought he would die when Ben pulled away from him. He didn't understand what happened until Ben lifted his legs and flipped him over, his hard cock never leaving Stefan's body. He lifted his arms and reached for Ben as the man began thrusting into him again.

As Ben leaned over him, he grasped that Ben knew what he needed. Ben looked into his eyes for several seconds before leaning closer and turning his head away, and bared his neck to Stefan.

"Now, baby," Ben groaned.

As Stefan sank his teeth into the side of Ben's neck, claiming him, he could feel Ben's cock swelling inside of him. He heard the deep roar of Ben's release as he thrust into him, the knot at the end of his cock extending to take hold deep inside of him again.

Stefan licked the small bite mark on the side of Ben's neck as he wrapped his arms around his shoulders, his hands grasping at his hair, stroking through the long black strands even as he tried to even out his breathing.

The only movement from Ben was the occasional quiver or small thrust. Stefan squeezed his knees against Ben's hips as he placed a trail of kisses along Ben's neck and jaw line. As the knot finally started to recede, Ben lifted his head and looked down at Stefan in wonder.

"I love the fact that you can't leave me for a while," Stefan whispered up at Ben as he brought his fingers up to gently stroke the side of Ben's face. "I like knowing I get to hold you for a little while afterwards."

* * * *

Ben smiled at Stefan, surprised at how much he seemed to smile since the little man came into his life. "I don't need the knot to be able to hold you, Stefan. I'll do it whenever I want to, knot or no knot."

Stefan giggled. "Yeah, but this way, you're still a part of me."

"You like me being a part of you?" Ben asked in amazement. No one had ever wanted to be a part of him before. He had been with others in the past, but usually they just wanted to be with him because of his size. Once they had, they soon left, not staying around to get to really know him.

"I think I could get used to it," Stefan laughed. "Of course, sometime I'd like to try this out in a bed. This table leaves something to be desired, you know?"

"Well," Ben said as he lifted Stefan up in his arms and stood to his feet. "I'm nothing if not accommodating."

Stefan laughed again as Ben pushed his jeans down his legs with his foot, then turned to carry him to the stairs. He wrapped his arms around Ben's neck and held on as Ben carried him up to their bedroom.

"Shower! We need to take a shower." Stefan laughed loudly as Ben started toward the bed. Ben immediately turned toward the bathroom, not releasing Stefan until they were standing in the shower, hot water spraying down on them.

Stefan groaned as Ben slid from his body. As Ben lowered him to the floor, his arms slid down from around his neck to rest on his chest. With a wicked little smile on his face, Stefan reached over and grabbed the body soap, pouring a liberal amount on a washcloth before replacing the bottle.

Stefan placed the washcloth on Ben's chest and began scrubbing him clean, not missing a single spot. As his hand moved farther down Ben's body, he knelt between his legs. He paid special attention to the soft, silky sac below Ben's cock, then all around the long flesh before him. He raised an eyebrow and looked up at Ben when his cock began to lengthen and harden right before his eyes.

"You do seem to have some amazing recuperative powers." He chuckled. "Are you always like this?"

"I…uh…well," Ben stammered. His face flushed. "I haven't been in the past. You might say this is a new development for me."

"That mating heat is a bitch, isn't it?" Stefan chuckled as he began washing Ben again.

"Stefan, it's not the mating heat," Ben replied, his eyes staring purposefully down at Stefan. He would have been aroused by Stefan even if they hadn't been mated.

Stefan looked up at Ben in surprise, then grinned, turning his attention back to washing Ben. Once he was done with the front, he motioned for Ben to turn around. Stefan seemed to take great delight in rubbing the cloth over every inch of Ben's ass, paying special attention to the area between his cheeks.

As he stroked the cloth over his small hole, Ben suddenly inhaled at the light touch. What impulse overtook Stefan, Ben would never know, but he would always be grateful as he felt Stefan place both of his hands on Ben's ass cheeks, pulling them apart.

"Sweet hell!" Ben shouted out as he felt Stefan's tongue swipe over his puckered hole. He pushed back with his ass, pressing Stefan's tongue against him. He moved his feet, widening the space between them until his feet were placed on the floor against each side of the shower.

He had never had anyone lick his ass before. Hell, he had never had anyone do anything with his ass before. In the past, he had always been on top. He had never had anyone make him feel the way Stefan did. It felt amazing.

"Stefan," he whispered, silently begging for more. He was rewarded with the quick swipe of Stefan's tongue again, and then the feeling of Stefan's tongue pressing gently against him. Ben thought his eyes were going to roll back into his head.

"Hand me the soap," Stefan said.

Ben stared down at him for a moment, confused until Stefan pointed to the bottle of body wash. "Hand me the soap," he said again.

Ben grabbed the soap and handed it to him, turning around to watch him pour a large amount onto his fingers. Once Stefan had closed the lid and set the bottle on the floor, he motioned for Ben to turn back around.

Ben turned around hesitantly, looking back over his shoulder even as he braced his hands against the shower wall. He could feel his muscles tighten up as Stefan spread his cheeks again and pressed a finger against his hole. He wasn't so sure about this. No one had ever been *there* before.

"Stefan—" he began.

"Relax, Ben. I know from earlier that this feels really good, believe me," Stefan said as he stroked the side of Ben's ass. "I wouldn't do anything you wouldn't like. Now, just relax for me, honey."

Ben turned around and leaned his head against the wall, taking several deep breaths as he tried to ease his muscles. He began to relax, only to clench right back up when Stefan pressed his finger against him again.

He continued to take several deep breaths as Stefan breached him, pressing one finger in and moving it around. Okay, that wasn't so bad, Ben thought as Stefan began pushing in and out with his finger.

As Stefan moved, he began relaxing more, the feeling turning from an invasive one to a pleasant sensation. He tensed just a little as Stefan added a second finger, scissoring the two back and forth. Okay, he could handle this.

"Turn around, honey," Stefan ordered.

Ben turned around, looking down at Stefan, his eyes falling closed when Stefan leaned forward and took his flagging cock into his mouth. Now, that felt good! Ben thought as he leaned back against the shower wall.

As Stefan took him deep into his mouth, he pushed his fingers into Ben's ass at the same time, moving them around until Ben jerked, crying out as his hands reached down to grasp at Stefan's hair.

"Fuck! What the hell was that?" Ben groaned as Stefan's finger brushed over his prostate again. He opened his eyes to look down at Stefan in shock. No wonder Stefan liked being on the receiving end. It was fantastic.

He saw Stefan smile around his cock just before his fingers brushed against his prostate again. Ben swore he could see stars explode behind his eyelids as he closed his eyes again and leaned his head back.

He was helpless to do anything but stand there and take what Stefan did to him. He was completely under his mate's control. His house could have been burning down, and he would have been unable to put out the fire. He was totally immersed in what Stefan did to him.

Stefan's mouth was moving back and forth along the long, thick, veined length of his cock. His tongue licked all over, up the sides, over the top, and along the slit in the top. Stefan's fingers were quickly pushing in and out, moving around to stroke against his sweet spot.

After coming twice just a little while before, Ben would have never thought it possible to do it again. He was wrong. As Stefan's tongue ran over the head of his cock, Ben felt his balls draw close to his body.

"Stefan, gonna—" Ben cried out as he erupted. He roared as he humped his hips against Stefan, feeling Stefan's fingers stroke against him over and over again. The pleasure just seemed to go on and on until his legs began to shake and he thought he would collapse on the shower stall floor.

As Stefan's mouth popped off of his cock, and he pulled his fingers free, Ben slid down to sit on the floor next to him. Ben reached out and grabbed him, pulling him against his wet body, holding him as close as he could without crushing his smaller form.

He took several deep breaths as he leaned down to brush his lips across the top of Stefan's head. He held Stefan for several minutes before chuckling down at him.

"See, baby, I don't need the knot to hold you."

Chapter 3

Stefan walked down the stairs a couple of days later, hoping to catch Ben before he went to work. He smiled when he heard swearing coming from the kitchen. Walking into the kitchen, he found Ben standing at the stove, a frying pan in one hand, a spatula in the other.

From the smoke rising from the stove, Stefan guessed that Ben was trying to cook something and not doing a very good job of it. As he walked closer, he winced at the state of the eggs in the pan. Ben was right. He couldn't cook.

"Here, give that to me," Stefan said as he reached for the pan and spatula. He pushed Ben aside with his shoulder, looking down at the mess in the pan before walking to the trashcan and dumping everything in. "Go get ready for work. I'll take care of this."

Walking back to the stove, he added some butter to the pan, then started cracking eggs into a bowl. Adding a little milk, he started whipping them together, and then poured them into the pan. As the eggs were cooking, Stefan went to the fridge and began searching around for stuff to add to the meal. Ben would not survive on a few eggs.

He found some ham, quickly slicing some up and adding it to the pan alongside the eggs. Finding some bread, he popped it in the toaster, putting butter and jam on the table. Once everything was cooked, he dished the food up on a plate and set it on the table.

"Ben, breakfast is ready," he called out as he poured two glasses of orange juice. He just sat down in his chair when Ben came walking in dressed in his deputy uniform. *Yum!* Stefan was pretty sure he was going to get a quick obsession with men in uniform.

Ben sat down at the table looking at the food before him with a little bit of awe. "How do you do this? I was just trying to make an egg and nearly burned the house down. This looks like a feast fit for a king, and you had it done by the time I got back downstairs."

Stefan shrugged his shoulders. "I like to cook."

Looking up at Stefan, Ben smiled. "Please, feel free to cook anything you want." He reached into his pocket and pulled out a small wad of cash, setting it on the table in front of Stefan. "Just in case you need anything from the store."

Stefan's hands trembled as he reached over and picked up the money. "I can use this?"

"Sure, buy whatever you need. If there's anything left over, get yourself something nice," Ben said as he took a bite of food. He closed his eyes as he chewed, opening them when he was done to look over at Stefan. "This is great, baby, thank you."

"It was nothing," Stefan replied as he stared at the money in his hand. He had never really had any money before. Oliver never let him have any. And here was Ben, handing him a wad of cash without even counting it.

"Don't you want to know how much is here?" Stefan asked quietly.

"I'm sure you'll put it to good use. Why? Do you need more?" Ben asked.

"No, I've just never had any money before. Oliver didn't allow me to have money."

"Oliver?"

"My stepbrother. He took care of all of our finances when our brother Desmond died."

"He wasn't the man trying to claim you, was he?"

Stefan shook his head. "No, that was Dane, Oliver's best friend, cohort, whatever you want to call him. Dane and Oliver have known each other for years. They pretty much do everything together."

"So, why was Dane trying to claim you then?" Ben asked.

"I guess they had some sort of arrangement or something. Dane got me, Oliver got Audley."

"Audley? Was he there that night?"

Stefan shook his head. "No, Oliver would never allow him to come to a mate gathering. There would be too much of a chance that someone else might claim Audley before he could. He's been obsessed with Audley since before I can remember."

"Where is Audley now?"

"I'm not real sure. I haven't been allowed to see him for a few weeks. Dane was supposed to claim me the other night, not you. When that didn't happen—" Stefan shrugged.

"Do you think he's in danger?" Ben asked.

"If Oliver claims Audley, yes. Oliver's not very…nice. He likes to get his own way and doesn't let others interfere with that. I'm surprised we haven't seen him before now. He's sure to be pissed over this," Stefan said as he gestured between the two of them.

"Not going to like having me for a brother-in-law, is he?" Ben chuckled.

"Uh, no!"

"Too damn bad," Ben growled, jumping to his feet and slamming his hands down on the table. "I claimed you fair and square. You belong to me now!"

Stefan stared at Ben in shock. No one had ever claimed him before. Ben sounded as if he really meant it, too. Stefan jumped up and launched himself around the table, jumping into Ben's arms.

"Just for that, I'm bringing you lunch," Stefan whispered in between kisses.

"For what?" Ben asked in confusion as he picked Stefan up in his arms.

Stefan raised his head, his hands framing Ben's face with his hands as he looked deep into his eyes. "For wanting me. No one's ever wanted me before. No one's ever claimed me before."

Ben smiled down at Stefan. "I have, and no one's going to take you away from me." He gave Stefan a quick kiss before setting him on the floor. "Breakfast was wonderful, baby, but I need to get to work. I'll expect lunch around one o'clock, okay?"

Stefan quickly nodded his head as he watched Ben grab one more bite of breakfast. A plan already started to form in his mind. He walked Ben to the front door and watched him leave, his mind going over what he needed to do to secure Audley's safety.

Getting Audley away from Oliver and Dane was very important to Stefan. Besides being Stefan's best friend, Audley had been the only thing that saved Stefan's sanity over the years. Stefan felt like he had a special connection to Audley, one that he never had with anyone else until he met Ben.

And just maybe his big bad wolf could help him save Audley. Ben was more caring than he thought. Stefan didn't care that everyone thought his mate was all big and bad. Ben wasn't. He was probably one of the most caring men Stefan had ever met, not that he had met a lot of caring people in his time. His life had been somewhat depressing until he met his mate.

But Stefan knew Ben had a lot of love to give. He also needed a lot of love. In just the small amount of time they had been together, Stefan could tell that Ben was soaking up the attention he received like a sponge. Stefan had no doubt that he could give Ben more love than he could handle. He just had to figure out how to get Ben to accept it.

* * * *

"Deputy Nobles, get your ass in my office ASAP!"

Ben rolled his eyes as he got up from his chair and walked into Sheriff Joe Nash's office. He closed the door and walked over to stand in front of Joe's desk, looking down at him expectantly.

"You bellowed?"

"Would you sit your ass down? You know it hurts my neck to have to look up at you," Joe growled as he gestured to the chair in front of his desk. "Now, tell me about the mate gathering the other night. I hear it was a real humdinger."

"I assume you've been talking to your father?" Ben asked as he sat down in a chair across from Joe.

Joe nodded his head, a wide grin on his face.

"Then what do you need to talk to me about?" Ben asked. "You already know what happened."

"Because I wanted to hear it from you."

Ben rolled his eyes as he settled back in his chair. "So, what do you want to know?"

"Is it true? Did you find your mate?" Joe asked, almost eagerly.

"Yes. His name is Stefan."

"When do we get to meet him?"

"He's bringing me lunch around one."

Joe nodded his head, sitting back in his chair and folding his hands together in his lap. "What's he like?"

"Stefan?" Ben shrugged. "I don't know. He's cute."

"Cute? You find a mate and all you can say about him is that he's cute?" Joe asked in astonishment.

Ben shrugged his shoulders. "It's only been a couple of days, Joe. I don't really know that much about him."

"Haven't you talked with him, asked him about his life, what he likes, dislikes?"

Ben could feel his face heating up as he looked down at his hands. "We haven't spent that much time…uh…talking."

He could hear Joe chuckling. "If it makes you feel any better, I was so obsessed with Nate, I didn't even know he could talk for nearly twenty-four hours."

Ben sat forward, resting his arms on his knees as he looked over at him. Joe Nash had been his best friend for more years than he could remember. When everyone else had been afraid of Ben because of his size, Joe couldn't have cared less.

"Is it always like that? I can't seem to stop thinking about him. Hell, we had sex so many times after I claimed him, I thought my balls would fall off. He walks into the room and I'm ready to rip off his clothes."

"Sorry to tell you this, but it's always like that and it doesn't go away. Nate can still get me going with just a phone call. If the city council knew how many times I've left work to run home and fuck my mate, I'd get fired for sure."

Ben chuckled. He couldn't help it. He could just picture Joe's little mate calling him on the phone and Joe running out of his office to go home. He had seen Joe tear out of here several times. He just never realized it was to go home and get frisky with Nate.

"So, basically, we're fucked?"

"Yeah," Joe said as he nodded his head. "That about covers it, my friend. If you think your size and demeanor means that you're going to be running things, think again. I'd lay bets that your new mate has you wrapped around his little finger inside of a week."

"I think he already does." Ben chuckled, remembering how Stefan had demanded that Ben claim him that first time. "You know, the first time I claimed him physically, he demanded that I do it? Just sat right down in my lap, pulled his clothes off, and demanded that I claim him."

Joe burst out laughing. "Sounds like a real fireball to me."

Ben smirked, shaking his head. "You have no idea."

"Well, congratulations, Ben. I hope he makes you very happy. I know I wasn't expecting Nate, but I couldn't imagine being with anyone else. He makes my life worth living. Besides that, he can cook like no one's business."

Ben started laughing—a very uncommon occurrence—and Joe looked slightly confused. "What?"

"Stefan loves to cook, and he's much better than I am. I was trying to make breakfast this morning when he rescued me. By the time I got back downstairs after getting ready for work, he practically had a feast on the table. I still don't know how he did it."

"Maybe you should introduce him to Nate. They can swap recipes or whatever it is that they do. Although, the two of them together does make me a little nervous. No telling what kind of trouble they could get into."

"Yeah, I'm not sure that's a good idea, but I know Stefan could use a friend. He had to leave his best friend behind when he mated me. I know he misses him."

"Why don't you have him over for dinner or to visit for a few days then? I'm sure it would make Stefan feel better," Joe asked.

Ben shook his head. "Stefan didn't go into a lot of detail, but there's some sort of issue involving his stepbrother, Oliver, and some guy named Dane. Apparently, Audley—Stefan's best friend—is Dane's little brother. Dane promised Audley to Oliver, and Dane was supposed to get Stefan. I kind of interfered with their plans."

"No shit? They were swapping siblings? Sounds a little fishy to me," Joe said, sitting forward in his chair. All of his former amusement had gone from his features. "Isn't he part of Prince Zacarius's coven?"

"You know, I don't think it ever came up. I'll have to ask Stefan when he gets here," Ben said. "Although, considering I met him at the mate gathering, I'd assume he is."

"You ask him and I'll make some discreet inquiries."

Ben nodded. "I'd appreciate it, Joe. It's weird, but I don't want Stefan unhappy."

"It's not weird, Ben. It's called having a mate. Weird is having a mate who's a sempath and can always tell if you're lying or not. Try building a relationship on that. I can't hide shit from that man."

Ben chuckled. He saw Nate using his unique abilities a time or two. It was a little eerie, but Joe seemed to dote on Nate's every word.

He wasn't freaked out by Nate's abilities, so Ben had decided early on that he wouldn't be either. Nate was just—Nate.

"I'm sure Stefan comes with his own baggage. I know I certainly do," Ben said, trying to make Joe feel a little better.

"Oh, don't get me wrong. I wouldn't give Nate up for anything. I just wish that sometimes I could get something past him. I can't even try to surprise him. He knows. He—" Joe stopped talking when there was a knock on the door. "Come in?"

Charlie stuck his head in, nodding to Joe before looking at Ben. "Uh, Ben, there's a guy out here. Says his name is Stefan and he's brought you lunch?"

Ben jumped to his feet and started to follow after Charlie, stopping to look back at Joe. "Do you need anything else, Joe?"

"No, Ben, go have lunch. But I expect you back here in an hour. No running home to have lunch, if you know what I mean."

"Hell, who needs to run home? A broom closet will work just fine." Ben chuckled as he walked out, shutting the door behind him. He immediately spotted Stefan standing by the door, looking around nervously.

Walking over, he wrapped an arm around him and leaned down to give Stefan a long, passionate kiss. "Hey, baby, what did you bring me for lunch?" he asked when he finally lifted his head.

"Ben," Stefan whispered, leaning in to take a deep inhale of his scent. Looking up at him, he smiled. "I missed you."

"It's only been a few hours, Stefan," Ben reminded him.

"And?"

Ben chuckled, getting a few strange stares from his fellow officers. He wasn't known for his sense of humor or for laughing. Stefan just seemed to bring it out in him. He said the most amazing things like they were the simplest words on the planet.

"So what's for lunch, baby?"

"Homemade chicken salad in pita pockets with fresh fruit salad and cherry cheesecake for dessert," Stefan said, holding up the sack in his hands.

"Mmm, my favorite," Ben said as he grabbed Stefan's hand and escorted him over to his desk.

"You've had chicken salad in pita pockets before?"

"No, but I can guarantee that as of today, it's my favorite. You've seen the way I cook, baby. Anything I would have brought from home could have given me food poisoning. How do you think I got this big?"

"Genetics?"

"Self preservation." Ben laughed as he sat down at his desk. "I needed a strong body to survive my own cooking."

Stefan laughed as he unpacked the bag of food he brought for Ben. "Oh, I see the way it is. You claimed me so you'd have someone to cook for you."

Ben grabbed Stefan around the waist and pulled him down onto his lap, his face nuzzling Stefan's neck. "It certainly wasn't because you're so damn sexy or the way my cock feels buried in your tight little ass, so it must be your cooking skills," Ben whispered into Stefan's ear.

Stefan giggled, wrapping his arms around Ben's neck. He leaned in and gave him a quick kiss. "Well, if you're really only after me for my cooking skills, I guess I should feed you. Need to keep you interested."

"Somehow, I don't think that is going to be a problem." Ben chuckled.

Stefan reached over, grabbed a container, and popped it open, handing Ben a pita pocket. Setting the container down on the desk, he quickly opened the others, then sat back in Ben's arms.

"Aren't you going to eat?"

Stefan shook his head. "I had enough to eat last night. I won't need any more for a couple of days. Werewolf blood gives me more nutrients than normal blood."

Ben stared for a moment, then nodded. "I guess I forgot about that. You'll let me know when you need to feed again, right?"

Stefan nodded. "It doesn't weird you out?"

"No, nothing about you weirds me out."

Stefan grinned. "I've heard there are a lot of ways for me to take blood, some of them are more erotic than others. Maybe next time I need to feed we can try them out."

Ben swallowed past the sudden lump in his throat. He could just imagine the many places Stefan could draw blood from. "Yeah, okay."

"You know I can only take blood from you now, right?" Stefan asked, a cautious look on his face. "If I drink blood from anyone else, it could kill me."

For some reason, that thought thrilled Ben. It made him feel like he had a special connection to Stefan that no one else in the world did, something more than mating. He could provide for his mate on a very basic level. The pride and possessiveness he felt at the thought made Ben lightheaded.

He wrapped his arm around Stefan to steady himself until the dizziness passed. Once the world righted itself, Ben smiled at Stefan. "I think I like that idea."

Ben could feel Stefan's gaze on him as he opened his mouth and took a piece of watermelon he held out. He slowly sucked the juices off Stefan's fingers. He pulled back to chew, smiling at the darkened and aroused look on Stefan's face.

"Looks like you got a better lunch than the rest of us, Ben. Gonna share?"

Ben glanced up to see Joe standing by his desk, an indulgent look on his face. Ben shook his head. "Nope. My baby made this all for me."

"Pig."

"Oink, oink." Ben laughed.

The man looked down at Stefan, holding out his hand. "I'm Sheriff Joe Nash. It's nice to meet you, Stefan. I've heard a lot about you."

Stefan looked at the hand before raising his head to glare at Joe. "Do you always refer to your deputies as pigs, sheriff?" Stefan asked bluntly.

Ben bit his lip to keep from laughing as he watched Joe turn a little red, shaking his head as he dropped his hand. "Uh, no, not normally. I didn't mean anything by it, Stefan. I was just—"

Stefan turned and looked at Ben when he couldn't hold his laughter back anymore. "And just what the hell are you laughing at?" he asked, cuffing Ben gently on the back of the head.

"Nothing, baby, I swear." Ben laughed as he held his hand out in front of him in surrender.

"Told you he'd be running things." Joe laughed as he crossed his arms over his chest and leaned back against the edge of Ben's desk. "Nate would have smacked me, too. Stefan, I apologize for calling your mate a pig. It won't happen again," Joe said as he looked down at Stefan.

Stefan turned to look up at the sheriff, nodding his head after several moments. "Who's Nate?"

"Nate is my mate. Ben mentioned that you like to cook. So does Nate. You might want to give him a call. I'm sure the two of you would have a lot to talk about," Joe said as he grabbed a pad of paper and wrote his phone number down on it.

"Here's our home phone. Nate is usually home most days, unless he's with my mother, who also likes to cook. Can I let him know you'll be calling?" Joe asked as he handed the paper to Stefan.

Stefan looked down at the paper for a moment, then tucked it away in his pocket. "I guess so, but I may need a few days. I'm still trying to get acclimated to my new surroundings. It took me forever just to find the sheriff's office."

"Nate was just passing through when we found each other. Now he knows every back road and short cut that there is. I'm sure you'll get used to it in no time, Stefan," Joe assured him.

Stefan nodded. He smiled at Joe as he watched him get to his feet.

"Don't forget to give Nate a call, Stefan. He'd be thrilled to meet you. I think it's hard for him with me being at work all day. I'm sure you know what I'm talking about."

Stefan nodded again. "Thank you, sheriff," Stefan replied.

"Please, call me Joe. Sheriff is just my job, not who I am."

"Joe, then." Stefan's smile grew a little bigger as Joe turned to leave, pausing for a moment to look back at Stefan curiously.

"Oh, hey, Stefan, Ben mentioned you met at the mate gathering the other night. Are you a member of Prince Zacarius's coven?"

"Yes. Why?" Stefan asked.

Ben could feel Stefan's apprehension in the tightening of his body. He wrapped his arms more fully around his mate, letting the man know he wouldn't let anything happen to him.

"Oh, no reason, really. I had a chance to meet your prince and was impressed by the man. He's made Devlin a very good mate, although I was sad to see Devlin leave Wolf Creek," Joe replied, shrugging his shoulders as he turned and walked away.

"So, interested in exploring the broom closet with me?" Ben asked as he nuzzled his face into Stefan's neck. Ben glanced at the man and wondered at his smile. What was he thinking? What had crossed his mind that would give him that strange smile? Was he thinking about what he would do to him once he got him alone?

He wasn't really thinking much else, considering all of the blood in his body had pooled in his groin. But he was feeling everything, especially the soft body held tight in his arms. Stefan squirmed a little on Ben's lap.

Ben groaned and reached into his desk drawer for the new bottle of lube he'd purchased on his way to work. He quickly shoved the tube into his pocket. Stefan's squirming drove him crazy. He needed to get them somewhere private and fast.

"Just how big is this broom closet?" Stefan murmured.

"Let me show you." Ben grinned as he grabbed Stefan and set him on his feet, standing up behind him. "Just walk in front of me. I don't want to scare the natives."

Stefan let out another giggle. He gave Ben a wicked smile as he brushed his hands against the bulge, giving him a little squeeze. "This might scare the natives, but I'm rather looking forward to it."

Ben growled. He quickly steered Stefan from the room and down the hallway. Ben's rapid stride stopped when he realized that the man he had been pulling behind him started to fall behind. Ben leaned down, picked the man up, and started carrying him.

Stefan seemed so light, Ben needed to check to make sure he was actually holding a person. The man weighed less than a bag of grain. But Ben could feel every soft curve resting against his chest.

Suddenly Ben had a need to get him away, not from prying eyes, but so that he could have Stefan to himself. He wanted to see Stefan's passion again, to see Stefan as he came unglued by Ben's touch.

He ignored the voice inside that said he was lying to himself. He really wanted to get Stefan alone so that he could claim his body, as well as his blood. Quickening his stride, he nearly ran down the hallway. A few minutes later, Ben pushed him into a small room lined with shelves, locking the door behind them.

Before Stefan could even turn around, Ben reached for his jeans, unbuttoning them and pushing them down off his feet. A moment later, he pressed Stefan up against the wall and took the man's hard cock deep inside his mouth.

"Oh, fuck, Ben," Stefan cried out above him.

Ben felt Stefan's hands clench in his hair. He didn't know exactly how much experience Stefan had. He didn't really want to know, but

Stefan seemed to love what Ben did to him. And Ben knew he loved being the one doing it.

"Ben, I can't—" Stefan cried out after only a moment. His hips pumped furiously against Ben. Stefan's hands tightened in Ben's hair to the point of pain. Ben ignored it and sucked harder, his cheeks hollowing out at the force of his suction.

His reward came moments later when Stefan stiffened. Then tangy cream filled Ben's mouth. Ben swallowed it all down, licking the long shaft, then around Stefan's balls until he cleaned up every last drop of the sweet liquid.

"Ben," Stefan said, his voice sounding all breathless.

Ben stood up and reached for the bottle of lube in his pocket. His hands shook as he popped the cap open and squirted a fair amount out on his fingers. He wanted nothing more than to sink his aching cock deep into Stefan's ass, but he knew he needed to prepare the man first. He'd never do anything to harm his little mate. He couldn't. It would be like slitting his own throat.

"Stefan, turn around and lean your hands against the wall."

Stefan turned and placed his hands on the wall. He pushed his ass out toward Ben and separated his legs. Ben's eyes just about glazed over. Stefan's little bubble butt was the sexiest damn thing he had ever seen.

Ben reached down and stroked his finger between Stefan's ass cheeks. The small shiver from Stefan almost brought Ben to his knees. Ben never thought he'd have something like this, someone made just for him. It felt intoxicating.

Ben leaned over and licked the side of Stefan's neck as he pushed his finger into Stefan's tight hole. "You're so damn responsive, baby," he whispered against Stefan's skin. "Do you know how much that turns me on?"

"Why don't you show me?" Stefan giggled and wiggled his butt.

Ben really didn't think Stefan had a clue how much he aroused Ben. Everything from the way he walked to the small twinkle in his voice when he laughed stirred up Ben to a fever pitch of desire that he found hard to control.

But Ben knew he needed to control his desire for Stefan. As small as his mate was, if Ben let loose the way he truly desired, Stefan could very easily be injured. Just the thought of hurting Stefan dampened Ben's lust enough for him to slow down a bit and regain control.

He pushed another finger into Stefan and started stretching him, his fingers moving back and forth, grazing the small walnut-sized button of pleasure that Ben knew drove his mate crazy. And he was correct. Stefan started pushing back against him, driving Ben's fingers deeper inside. His breath came out in small pants.

"Ben," Stefan begged. "Please, I need you."

"Not yet, baby," Ben said, fighting his instinct to give in to Stefan's plea. "You're not ready for me. Just one more finger to go." Ben pushed in another finger. Stefan's body seemed to suck him right in. Ben couldn't wait to feel the same thing happen to his cock.

Ben stepped slightly to the side of Stefan and reached down with his free hand to grab Stefan's cock. Surprise made him look down. Stefan's cock was already hard again. Drops of pre-cum glistened on the mushroomed head.

Ben stroked Stefan's cock with one hand and pushed his fingers into the man's ass with the other. Stefan started rocking back and forth, driving his cock into Ben's grip, then impaling himself on Ben's fingers. The little pants coming from his throat turned to groans.

"Ben, please. I'm ready."

So was Ben. He pulled his fingers free of his mate and spun the man around to pick him up. He pushed Stefan back against the wall, the last of his control slipping away at the need blazing across Stefan's face.

Ben held Stefan with one arm and unbuttoned his pants with the other. He had just enough time to push his pants down his thighs before desperate need overtook him and he thrust into Stefan.

He stiffened and closed his eyes, momentarily speechless at the feeling of warm silk that encircled him. He'd been inside of Stefan a number of times since they mated, but each instance felt like the first time. And each one felt better than the last one. If this kept up, Ben knew he'd be dead before the year was out.

Could a man die from being oversexed?

"Ben," Stefan whispered.

Ben opened his eyes and looked down at Stefan. He grinned. "What do you need, baby?"

Stefan's eyes dropped down to Ben's throat. Ben's heart thudded. He knew what Stefan wanted. It made his blood boil in his veins. He had no idea how being bitten by a vampire turned into something sexual, but it had. The mere thought made him start thrusting into Stefan.

Ben gripped Stefan's hips in his hands and tilted his head to one side. His breath quickened when he felt Stefan's tongue brush across his skin. Ben braced himself. The momentary pain he felt when Stefan's canines sank into his flesh quickly turned to one of overwhelming pleasure.

Ben dug his fingers into Stefan's ass. He thrust harder. He worried that he would leave bruises on his mate, but he couldn't seem to stop himself from pounding into the smaller man. The more Stefan sucked on his neck, the more Ben lost control until he was mindless with desire.

Stefan suddenly tossed his head back and cried out. Hot liquid splashed between them, covering Ben's stomach and chest. The sweet smell of his lover's release was all Ben needed to toss him over the edge into orgasmic bliss. The tightening of Stefan's inner muscles around his throbbing cock was just an added bonus.

"Stefan!" Ben roared as he filled his little mate with his seed, possessing him on the inside even as he possessed him on the outside by sinking his teeth into the soft skin between Stefan's neck and shoulder.

The knot took hold, keeping Ben and Stefan tied closely together. Ben's legs trembled. He pulled his teeth from Stefan's neck and wrapped his arms around the man's body as he sank to his knees.

Ben took big gulps of air into his empty lungs. He felt Stefan's hand stroking his hair and raised his head to look down at him. He worried that he might have hurt Stefan until he saw the happy serene smile on his face.

"Hey, baby, you okay?" Ben murmured. "I didn't hurt you?"

"I'm great," Stefan whispered back. "How are you?"

"A little weak in the knees." Ben chuckled. Ben leaned into the hand that Stefan stroked over his cheek.

"I like that."

"Like what?" Ben asked, confused.

Stefan grinned. "Knowing I can bring you to your knees."

"I suspect that there are a lot of things you're going to like over the years," Ben said as he stood to his feet. His legs wobbled a bit, but he had enough strength to lower Stefan carefully to the floor. "I don't seem to have any resistance to you."

"Are you saying that's a bad thing?" Stefan asked as he fixed his clothes.

"No, but I suspect our lunches need to be few and far between, or I won't get any work done." Ben pulled his pants up and buttoned them. He grinned over at Stefan. "How am I supposed to concentrate on work with your sexy ass hanging around?"

"You could always come home early."

Ben snorted. He could just picture himself running out of the sheriff's office the way Joe did when Nate called. Somehow, the idea didn't seem so bad to him. He could see himself doing exactly that.

Ben opened the door and smacked Stefan on the ass as he walked by. "Lunch is at one o'clock tomorrow. I expect to see you then."

Chapter 4

Stefan bounced from foot to foot as he watched out the window, waiting for Ben to get home from work. Over the last few weeks, Stefan had grown to love the time when Ben came home from work. It usually led to some more interesting, and slightly sweaty, activities. This time, though, worry filled Stefan as he waited.

He'd talked to Devlin on the phone, just wanting to check in with his old coven, and heard the news from the Prince's consort that Oliver was preparing to claim Audley in a commitment ceremony. They needed to do something before that happened.

Audley and Stefan had been friends for years. Besides Ben and Devlin, Stefan couldn't think of anyone he felt closer to in the world. He couldn't leave Audley to face Dane and Oliver alone, not when he might be able to do something about the situation.

Stefan's heart thudded when Ben's truck pulled up in front of the house. He twisted his hands together nervously in front of him as he waited for the man to reach the front door. His mind congested with doubts and fears.

What if Ben said no? What if he got mad? What if Ben didn't want to go after Audley? All of the scenarios running through Stefan's head were a very real possibility. The longer it took for Ben to reach the house, the more scared Stefan became.

Finally, the front door opened and Ben walked in, a large smile on his face. Stefan couldn't help but smile back. The more time they spent together, the more Ben seemed to smile. Stefan hoped it was due to him.

"Hey, baby," Ben said. "How was your day?"

"Better now that you're home." Stefan's nervousness of a few minutes ago disappeared in the face of the man who stood before him. Stefan launched himself across the room and threw himself into Ben's arms, his lips searching desperately for his mate's.

"I think someone missed me," Ben said against Stefan's lips.

"I did miss you," Stefan assured his mate. "If I could figure out how you could work from home, I would." If Stefan had his way, Ben would never leave, not only because Stefan hated his mate being gone all day long, but because he worried about him.

"It's only been a couple of weeks since I claimed you, Stefan," Ben replied. "Haven't you gotten used to me being gone to work by now?"

Stefan rubbed Ben's chest. "I hope I never get used to it."

"You know what I do is dangerous, but I take every precaution, I promise," Ben said. "I would never do anything that might jeopardize what we have. Surely you know that? I've been both the deputy here in Wolf Creek and a pack soldier for a long time, Stefan."

Stefan pouted. He fiddled with the edge of Ben's shirt collar. "I know that. I just worry." He glanced up at Ben. "There's someone else I worry about, too." Okay, it wasn't a great way to bring up the subject of Audley, but Stefan knew he needed to do it somehow.

"Audley?"

Stefan's mouth dropped open. He stared up at Ben for a moment, shock coursing through him, then snapped his mouth shut. "Yeah, how'd you know?"

Ben chuckled, another sound that Stefan had heard a lot of lately. He patted Stefan on the ass, then walked past him. "I know you, Stefan. You haven't mentioned your friend in several days. If you truly cared about someone, you wouldn't forget about them."

Stefan felt his face burn. He frowned as he followed Ben upstairs to the bedroom and watched him change his clothes. Ben always headed directly to the bedroom to change out of his uniform and get into something more comfortable. He usually chose jeans and a cotton shirt. Stefan would have preferred naked skin, but the tight jeans worked, too.

"Want to tell me about it?" Ben asked as he pulled a white cotton shirt over his head.

Stefan sat down on the side of the bed. "I talked with Devlin today. He told me that Oliver is planning a commitment ceremony to Audley." He heaved a deep sigh and clasped his hands tightly together. "I know Audley, Ben. He would never agree to be committed to Oliver. He's terrified of my brother."

Ben smoothed his shirt down then stepped over to sit next to Stefan. "So, what should we do, baby? Can't we just go get Audley? Would he come with us if we asked? We have a spare bedroom he can use as long as he wants."

Stefan shook his head. "It's not that easy, Ben."

"Why not?" Ben asked. "I admit I don't know much about vampire culture, but if Audley is old enough to do what he wants—" Ben paused for a moment, a strange look crossing his face. "He is old enough, isn't he?"

"Audley is the same age as me."

Ben frowned. "You're old enough, aren't you? I know you guys live a long time, but you mature just like the rest of us, right? I'd hate to find out that I'm robbing the cradle here, Stefan."

"You're not." Stefan laughed. "I'm plenty old enough. Vampires mature just like everyone else until we hit puberty. Only then does our aging start to slow down. And now that we're mated, your life thread is intertwined with mine and you'll live as long as I do."

"And that means what exactly?" Ben asked. "Am I going to turn into a vampire?"

"No, of course not," Stefan replied. He chuckled at the anxious look on Ben's face. "Werewolves are immune to a vampire bite. You will live as long as I do. However, you will also die when I do or vice versa. If you die, so do I."

"Seriously?"

Stefan nodded. "Does that bother you? Being with me for so long, I mean?"

"No, baby, not at all," Ben said. Stefan squeezed Ben's hand when the man grabbed him. "In fact, I prefer it that way. I just worry about you, maybe as much as you worry about me. My job can get kind of dangerous sometimes, and I'd hate to think of something happening to you because of me."

Stefan leaned over to bump his shoulder against Ben's. "Guess you'll just have to be extra careful, won't you?"

Ben growled. Stefan squealed when the large man picked him and settled him down on his lap. Stefan wrapped his arms around Ben, leaning in to inhale the musky scent at Ben's neck. He knew if he were a cat, he'd be purring. Ben smelled delicious.

"I guess I will need to be extra careful," Ben said. His arms wrapped around Stefan. "I'm holding my life in my arms."

* * * *

Stefan could feel the difference in the atmosphere as they drove up the driveway of Prince Zacarius's estate. It wasn't cold exactly, but more like a sudden foreboding chill that ran up Stefan's spine and made him shiver.

"Ben?" he whispered.

"Yeah, baby?"

"Do you feel that?"

"Feel what, baby?"

Stefan shook his head. He couldn't put his finger on it, but something felt off. Could it be coming back to coven territory? Or was it something more sinister? Whatever it was, Stefan just wanted to get his stuff and Audley and get back to Wolf Creek.

"Stefan?"

"Something feels wrong, Ben."

"Do you want to turn around and head back home?"

"No," Stefan said, trying to bolster his courage. "We need to find Audley and get this over with."

"Does it bother you being back here?" Ben asked as he brought their truck to a stop and turned the engine off. "Is it the coven?"

"No, I don't think so. Prince Zacarius has always been a good leader. He cares for the members of his coven. Since he mated with Devlin, though, he's a lot more…I don't know…personable? He gets a lot more involved in the lives of those in the coven."

Ben chuckled. "Devlin can do that to a person. Mind you, I didn't get long to know the man before he mated your prince, but he always seemed liked an exceptional man."

"Devlin's cool." Stefan frowned. "He didn't even get real mad at me when he found out I poisoned the prince."

"You poisoned the prince?"

Stefan felt his face drain of color at the shock in Ben's voice. He might have forgotten to tell his mate that little tidbit of information. "Um, yeah, but I didn't mean it." Stefan tilted his head to the side. "Well, at the time I did, but I meant to poison Devlin, not Prince Zacarius. It just didn't turn out quite like I planned."

"Why would you try to poison Devlin?"

"I thought he would try to kill my prince. I couldn't let that happen." Stefan turned to look at Ben, desperately hoping he could make the man understand what he needed to say. "You have to understand, I was raised in a household that fully supported the war between vampires and werewolves. I'd always been taught that werewolves were monsters. I truly thought Devlin came to kill Prince Zacarius and I couldn't let that happen."

Ben just stared.

"I know that it's not true now and I swore to Devlin and Prince Zacarius that I would never do something like that again," Stefan said quickly. He squirmed a little in his seat. His fingers plucked at a stray fabric string on his jeans. "I know it was wrong."

"Sweet Jesus, Stefan. You're full of surprises."

Stefan grimaced. That didn't sound very reassuring. Stefan didn't know if Ben would hate him now or not. Trying to kill someone—especially the leader of his people—was pretty big stuff. Ben enforced the laws of his people. Stefan didn't know if his mate would understand that it had all been a misunderstanding.

"You really tried to kill Devlin?"

Stefan nodded, watching Ben carefully through the fall of his hair.

Ben chuckled. "I think I would have paid to see the expression on Devlin's face when he found out about that."

Stefan frowned. That wasn't the response he expected. "He wasn't real happy about it."

"I imagine not." Ben laughed some more as he opened his door and climbed out.

Stefan watched him come around the truck until the man opened his door. Ben certainly didn't seem to be bothered by what he did, more like amused. "You're not upset?"

"Well, I don't think you should go around poisoning people, Stefan," Ben said. "But if anyone deserved it, Devlin did. The man's a pain in the ass."

"Hey," said an offended-sounding voice from behind them. "I resent that."

"I do, too," said another voice. This one sounded much more amused. "Devlin never caused me a moment of pain in *my* ass."

Stefan felt his face flame as he looked around Ben to see Devlin and Prince Zacarius standing at the bottom of the steps leading into the mansion. Stefan quickly jumped from the truck and moved around Ben. He bent his head, bowing respectfully.

"Prince Zacarius."

He heard a low growl from behind him before large hands picked him up. Stefan's startled yelp was smothered by the hard body he was pressed against and the arms wrapped around his waist holding him off the ground.

"Ben!" Stefan exclaimed.

"Mine!" Ben growled. His voice was hard and possessive, and it thrilled Stefan down to his very toes. He grinned over at Devlin and the prince. Devlin laughed and looped an arm around Zacarius's shoulders.

"Dude, you don't think I have my hands full with my own mate?" Devlin asked. "What in the hell would I do with another one? I have a hard enough time keeping track of this one."

Stefan felt Ben slowly loosen the arm he held around his waist. He was lowered to the ground, but Ben didn't stop hovering or release his hold. Stefan giggled and settled his body back against Ben's, content to be right where he was.

"I'm not sure I like the idea that you think you have to keep track of me," Prince Zacarius griped. "Just who's the prince here? Hmmm? I thought I was the one in charge."

Stefan's eyes widened in shock as Devlin grinned at Prince Zacarius.

"Let's get Stefan and Ben settled in their room," Devlin said. "Then I'll show you who's in charge."

Prince Zacarius's face flushed, but Stefan doubted the man felt embarrassed. His arousal saturated the air around them. Stefan wiggled in Ben's arms. He felt a little weird witnessing the intimate play between the prince and his royal consort, mostly because he found it arousing.

Stefan didn't know how he felt about that. He'd never imagined watching other people have sex and being aroused by it. It wasn't that he relished the idea of watching Devlin and his mate fuck, just the intimate contact between two people that truly cared about each other. Stefan found that interplay fascinating.

He wondered if he and Ben looked as happy as Devlin and Prince Zacarius did when they loved on each other. He hoped so. Stefan knew neither he nor Ben had made declarations of undying love to each other. Didn't mean he didn't feel it. He just hoped Ben did, too.

"Have you heard anything new from Audley?" Stefan asked, breaking up the uncomfortable silence that fell over the group.

Devlin looked up, startled, then shook his head. "There's been nothing new since I talked to you last. Zacarius sent out a message yesterday requesting Audley's presence here at the mansion. He's supposed to be here tonight."

"Is Oliver or Dane coming with him?" Stefan asked. Just the thought made him shiver and lean closer to Ben. He felt gratitude flow through him when Ben tightened his arm and pulled him closer.

"I imagine Dane will, at the least," Prince Zacarius said. "You know Audley is under Dane's control until he's mated."

Stefan didn't like it, but he knew the prince was right. Until Audley's mate claimed him and took responsibility for him, he had to do as Dane said. It sucked. It sucked when Stefan was under his stepbrother's thumb too.

"Come on inside, you two," Devlin said. "At least we can get you settled while we wait."

"I'll get your bags, young sir."

"Albert!" Stefan exclaimed. He pushed himself away from Ben and toward Prince Zacarius's manservant. He wrapped his arms around the man and hugged him. "I've missed you so much."

Albert graced Stefan with one of his rare smiles. "You've been missed as well, young sir."

Stefan heard another low growl. He rolled his eyes, dropped his arms from around Albert and stepped back into Ben's waiting arms. He was instantly pulled back against Ben's hard body. He patted Ben's arm.

"Albert, meet my mate, Ben Nobles," Stefan said. "He's a deputy in Wolf Creek. Ben, this is Albert, Prince Zacarius's manservant. He's been with the prince longer than even I have been alive."

Albert seemed to assess Ben as he looked him up and down. Apparently he liked what he saw because he nodded and gave Ben a small bow of his head. "Mr. Nobles, welcome to Prince Zacarius

Ivinovav's coven estate. If there is anything I can do to make your stay more comfortable, please do not hesitate to ask. I am at your disposal."

Stefan blinked. That was a mouthful. He wasn't sure he'd ever heard Albert talk so much to a complete stranger and a werewolf at that.

"Just remember what belongs to me and we'll be fine," Ben said.

"I understand perfectly, sir, and that is as it should be," Albert replied. "I'll get your bags from the vehicle, if I may?"

Once Ben nodded, Albert swept past them and headed for the truck. A moment later, he came back and walked right past everyone carrying two large bags in his hands. He nodded to the prince, then went inside.

"I believe Albert has you in the blue room, Stefan," Prince Zacarius said. "I'm sure you remember the way. If you'd like to freshen up, dinner will be served at seven o'clock."

"Will Audley be here for dinner, your highness?" Stefan asked as he and Ben followed them inside the large mansion.

"He was not requested to come to dinner, but if he is still here, then I see no reason why he could not join us," Prince Zacarius replied.

Stefan bit his lip for a moment as he considered whether or not to ask the prince for more than he already received. The prince had been very understanding about Stefan's worry over Audley. It would be rude to ask for more.

"Stefan?"

"I was wondering if there was any way that I could have a few minutes alone with Audley," Stefan asked. He twisted his hands together at the puzzled look on the prince's face. "Audley is horribly shy, your highness. I'm not sure he'd tell you if anything was wrong, but he might tell me."

Prince Zacarius nodded. "I'm sure something can be arranged."

"Thank you, your highness," Stefan said, feeling overwhelming relief. "You don't know how much this means to me. With the exception of Ben, Audley is my best friend. I'd be devastated if anything happened to him."

Stefan grew worried when the prince's eyebrow shot up. Had he said something wrong? Insulted the prince in some way? He thought back over his words, but found nothing wrong with what he'd said.

"You consider your mate your best friend?"

"Of course." Stefan frowned. "Don't you?"

The prince chuckled and reached over to take Devlin's hand in his. "I never really thought about it, but I suppose you are correct, Stefan. I'm just surprised you've come to this conclusion after being mated for so little time."

Stefan felt the sudden urge to defend his mate. "Ben is more than my mate, your highness," he said stiffly.

"Oh?"

"He protects me as a mate should, true, but there's a lot more than that involved," Stefan insisted as he walked next to the prince. "He worries about me. If I'm warm enough. If I've had enough to eat. If I'm happy. He lets me know on a daily basis that I'm the most important person in the world to him. His strength and size are just an added bonus."

"Yes, I can see where his strength and size would be an asset to any leader," the prince replied. "But that doesn't leave much room for anything else, now does it?"

Stefan felt rage boil through his body. The prince didn't understanding what Stefan was trying to say. No one saw Ben as he did, and he couldn't understand why.

"He wouldn't hurt a fly unless he needed to, and it's time that people like you saw him as more than cannon fodder for your battles. Ben is smart, handsome, and loving," Stefan snapped. He stopped walking and planted his hands on his hips as he glared at Prince Zacarius.

Stefan took a deep breath, ignoring the stunned looks aimed in his direction, and continued. "Everyone seems to think less of Ben because of the battle scars on his body. I see them as a sign of the courage and bravery that are a natural part of Ben's personality." Stefan gestured over toward his mate. "He received those scars defending his pack, the people he loves. He should have medals for each one of them. They mean that he defended his pack and that someone lived because of what he did. Ben is the sweetest, most gentle person I have ever met. And I'm tired of you people seeing him as some sort of monster!"

* * * *

Ben stared at Stefan, stunned by the words coming out of his mate's mouth. He couldn't believe Stefan thought that way about him. He also couldn't believe that Stefan was practically yelling everything at the prince of his former coven.

"He's good," Devlin whispered.

Ben turned to stare at Devlin.

"He obviously cares deeply for you, Ben," Devlin continued. "I'm glad. I hoped the two of you would hook up after I met Stefan. I thought at the time he needed your strength, but now I'm beginning to wonder if he's not the stronger of the two of you."

Devlin chuckled and crossed his arms over his chest as he watched his mate and Stefan. "He certainly seems hell bent on defending you."

Yeah, he is. He couldn't ever remember anyone defending him quite like Stefan did. It grabbed a small part of Ben, deep inside, and made it glow just for the little man. Ben grinned. "He's mine."

Not able to stand the separation a moment longer, Ben reached over and grabbed Stefan by the arm and yanked his mate into his arms. He heard a small yelp fall from Stefan's lips a moment before he covered them with his own, kissing the man until all resistance fell away and Stefan kissed him back.

When Ben finally lifted his head a few moments later, they were alone in the entryway of the mansion. Ben looked down at Stefan, excited by what he saw. Stefan's face looked flushed, his lips wet and swollen. His sky-blue eyes looked dazed. Stefan looked like sex incarnate.

"Where's that blue room, baby?"

Stefan pointed to the stairway across the room. "Upstairs," he whispered.

Ben grinned and swept his mate up in his arms, quickly walking toward the stairs. He couldn't have cared less that they were smack dab in the middle of a vampire coven mansion or that his mate just chewed the coven prince out. He didn't even care that they were there on a mission to save Stefan's best friend.

Ben's only concern at the moment was finding that damn blue room they were staying in, getting Stefan naked as fast as he could, and introducing them both to the wonders that could be found in a bed.

Or against a wall.

On a countertop.

The floor.

Ben wasn't picky. Any flat surface would do.

* * * *

Stefan's heart thudded in his chest. He twisted his hands together until he realized what he was doing. Dropping them down to his sides, he started plucking at the soft material of his slacks as he paced around the room.

He was nervous and scared. The only thing that kept him from totally losing it was the large, silent form who stood by the window, watching him freak out. He adored Ben—really, he did—but the man had never had a best friend before and didn't understand why Stefan felt concerned.

"Baby, calm down," Ben said. "You're going to make yourself sick."

Stefan shook his head. "I can't. I know Prince Zacarius can order Audley in here alone, but either Oliver or Dane could cause quite a stink about it. I don't want to cause the prince any problems. He has enough without my shit."

"Stefan, your prince is just as concerned about this situation as you are. I'm sure he doesn't mind helping you out. He's the prince of your coven, baby. He understands these things."

Stefan turned to watch his mate cross the room to him. Ben insisted on being there when Stefan met up with Audley. Stefan couldn't say no to his mate, especially not after the previous night. Ben had rocked Stefan's world and then cradled him close as if he were the most precious thing in the world. If Stefan hadn't already been in love with Ben, he would have fallen then.

"Everything is going to be okay, baby," Ben said softly.

Stefan closed his eyes and leaned into the hand Ben stroked down his face. How anyone could ever think his mate was anything but a kind, gentle man, he didn't know. It showed every time Ben touched him.

Stefan opened his eyes and looked up at his mate. He tried to put everything he felt for the big man in his eyes. "I love you, Ben."

Ben's breathing hitched. His eyes widened. The deep golden color in them shined brighter until it looked like sunshine. Stefan saw Ben blink several times as moisture seemed to gather in the corners. He opened his mouth as if to say something, then snapped it close.

Stefan smiled. He reached up and cupped the side of Ben's face. "You're more than just a mate to me. You're the man I want to spend the rest of my life with. You mean the world to me, Ben, and I will love you until I die." A single tear trailed down Ben's cheek. Stefan wiped it away with his finger. "I'll spend the rest of my life proving it to you if I have to."

Ben chuckled. "You don't," he whispered. "I've just never had anyone tell me that they loved me before. I don't think anyone *has* ever loved me before."

"I do."

"I believe you."

"I just hope that someday you'll feel the same," Stefan murmured.

"I feel something, Stefan. I'm just not sure what it is." Ben grimaced. "I don't know much about love. I've never had it before. I need to wait until I know, okay? Just give me a little more time, baby."

Stefan nodded. "I'll give you all of the time you need. I'm not going anywhere."

Ben grinned and hugged him. Stefan buried his face in Ben's chest. His heart ached to hear words of love from Ben, but he knew he couldn't force them. Ben would tell him when he was ready and not before. Stefan would just have to be patient.

"You're my mate, Stefan," Ben said softly, "but more than that, I want you to be my mate. I don't want anyone else."

Stefan smiled, tightening his grip around Ben. It was enough for now. Stefan pushed back from Ben, ready to tell him so when he heard voices coming down the hallway. He turned to look at the door, his heart pounding again.

"Looks like your friend is here, baby," Ben said. "I'm going to go stand over here by the window so I don't scare him, okay?"

Stefan nodded, not really paying attention to Ben. Audley was here.

* * * *

Ben chuckled to himself as he went to sit on the window sill. Stefan was practically vibrating as he waited for the door to open. He knew Stefan and Audley were close—were best friends—but his little mate looked like he was about to shake apart.

The blue of his eyes dominated his beautiful heart-shaped face. His delicate little hands twisted together again. Ben knew if Stefan started fidgeting with his pants once again, he might wear a hole in them. The man was so nervous.

The door opening and a small figure being ushered into the room by Albert caught Ben's attention. Of course, he recognized Albert. The small man, though, Ben had never seen before in his life. But he suddenly wanted to. Audley Ebane was stunning.

"If you will just wait here, young sir, the prince will call for you when he's done with his meeting," Albert said before slipping out of the room.

Ben suddenly knew where Stefan got his nervousness from when Audley began to twist his hands together. He heard a loud cry from Stefan, then his mate flew across the room to hug the smaller man, smaller than even Stefan.

"Oh my God, Audley," Stefan cried. "I didn't think I'd ever see you again."

"Stefan," Audley whispered, his voice as light as a bird's chirp. "Is it really you? Dane said you betrayed the coven and got exiled."

Stefan chuckled. "No, I met my mate at the mate gathering a few weeks ago. Dane was there and tried to claim me, but Ben got to me first."

Audley's hand covered his mouth and his face paled. "That's why Dane was so mad. He expected to mate you."

Stefan nodded. "Would you like to meet my Ben?"

Ben tried to look smaller when Stefan gestured to him. He didn't want to frighten Audley, but he sure wouldn't mind getting closer to him. He hadn't been this fascinated with someone since he saw Stefan for the first time. He couldn't understand it or the feelings of possessiveness filling him.

"Ben?" Stefan asked. "Come meet Audley."

Ben walked slowly across the room. He could see the fear in Audley's eyes. It wasn't anything he didn't expect. Most people were afraid of him—well, everyone except Stefan. He stopped next to Stefan and held out his hand.

"Hello, Audley," he said as softly as he could. "It's nice to finally meet you. Stefan has told me a lot about you."

* * * *

Audley swallowed past the sudden lump that took hold in his throat at the sight of the biggest man he'd ever seen in his life. He reached out to shake the man's hand, surprised at the gentleness of Ben's grip.

"Hello, Ben," Audley replied. "Stefan hasn't told me anything about you."

Audley just barely caught himself from jumping when the man's chest rumbled with his laughter. He dropped the hand Ben held out to him and stepped back. Audley couldn't help but wonder how Stefan found himself mated to such a man.

"You're really mated?" he asked, his heart aching.

Stefan nodded. The huge grin on his face matched the one on Ben's face. Audley felt sorrow bang at the walls of his heart. He had always dreamed he and Stefan might be mated one day. It was often the only thing that kept Audley going when things got tough.

Audley tried to bolster himself with the knowledge that at least Stefan had someone strong who would care for him, protect him. That was something. Audley smiled. "I'm glad for you, Stefan."

"Come, sit down," Stefan said. "Prince Zacarius has arranged for us to have a little time alone."

Audley glanced over his shoulder at the door. "Oh, I don't know. Dane and Oliver will be looking for me."

"No, Prince Zacarius said he'd keep them occupied for a while, give us some time to catch up." Stefan plopped down in a chair and gestured for Audley to sit down. "Have a seat."

Audley sat down across from Stefan. His eyes strayed to Ben, watching him walk to a crystal decanter sitting on a sideboard. He watched Ben begin to pour three drinks before turning his attention back to Stefan.

"So, tell me everything that's happening," Stefan said. He smiled when Ben handed him one of the glasses of alcohol. "The royal consort told me that Dane and Oliver are going ahead with the mating ceremony. Is that true?"

Audley nodded. He started to reach for the glass Ben held out to him when he heard a deep growl. The glass slipped through Audley's fingers and fell to the floor, breaking into several pieces.

Audley groaned. He was always such a klutz. He reached down to start picking up the pieces of glass as Ben knelt down to do the same. Startled, Audley didn't pay attention to what he was doing and picked up a piece of broken glass.

He winced as the glass cut into his hand, dropping it with a small hiss and yanking his hand to his chest. "Ouch!"

"Did you cut yourself?" Ben asked, moving over to kneel in front of him. It didn't seem to matter if he knelt or not, Ben still stood taller than Audley. "Here, let me see."

Audley held his bleeding hand out to Ben, unable to resist his quiet command. Luckily, it didn't seem to be a large cut. It just bled a lot. Ben held his hand carefully, examining the cut with his fingers.

"Well," Ben said after a moment. "It doesn't look too bad. We just need something to stop the bleeding. Stefan, can you find something?"

Audley glanced up to see Stefan jump up from his chair to start searching the room for something to cover Audley's hand. He suddenly felt something warm brush across his hand. Audley looked down.

Audley's mouth dropped open and shock welled through him. Ben was licking the blood off his hand, and he looked happy as fuck doing it. Audley didn't know if he felt scared or something worse.

The sight of Ben's tongue brushing across his hand seemed to have a direct connection to his cock. Every swipe against his skin felt like a stroke on his suddenly interested shaft. The low growl from Ben didn't help matters much.

Feeling like he had totally betrayed his friendship with Stefan by feeling aroused by the man's mate, Audley yanked his hand away and cradled it to his chest. His eyes shot to Stefan, widening when he saw Stefan just staring at Ben with a confused expression on his face. It bordered on hurt.

"Ben?" Stefan murmured. "What are you doing?"

"Christ, Stefan," Ben gasped. He leaned forward and grabbed Audley's wrist, holding it out toward Stefan. "Taste this, damn it."

Stefan frowned, but stepped forward and raked his tongue across the cut on Audley's hand. Audley trembled as Stefan's eyes fell closed and the man groaned as if he had just tasted ambrosia.

Audley glanced up at Ben to see his reaction, only to find the man staring at him intently. It unnerved Audley and made him feel like Ben knew something he didn't. He pulled on his arm, trying to wrest it from Stefan's grasp.

"Stefan, please," Audley pleaded.

Stefan finally released him and Audley pulled away, scooting back into his chair as far as he could. He cradled his hand in his lap and looked from Stefan to Ben in confusion. "What's going on?"

Stefan glanced over his shoulder up to Ben. The big man just shrugged his shoulders. "He's your friend," Ben said. "You tell him."

Audley wasn't sure he wanted to hear what Stefan had to say when the man turned back to face him. The resigned look on Stefan's face didn't help matters much. It didn't provoke confidence in Audley. In fact, it scared the crap out of him.

"Stefan?" he whispered.

Stefan patted Audley's leg. "It's okay, Audley. It's not a bad thing."

"What isn't?" Audley cried out. "What are you talking about?"

"When Ben licked the blood off your hand, he discovered something, something very important," Stefan said. "He wanted me to taste your blood to confirm his suspicions and he's right."

"Please, just tell me," Audley begged. "Am I dying?"

"Oh God, no, Audley," Stefan said. He stood up and stepped closer, his arms encircling Audley. Ben instantly took Stefan's place, kneeling behind Stefan at Audley's feet. "It's nothing like that, I swear."

"You're safe, little one," Ben said softly.

"Don't you see, Audley?" Stefan asked as he released Audley and stepped over to kneel down next to Ben. "You're our mate."

Chapter 5

Ben watched a variety of emotions cross Audley's face, everything from fear to disbelief to a touch of hope. He imagined the man felt much like he did when he discovered Stefan was his mate and claimed him.

Ben reeled from the knowledge that he had two mates, not one. It didn't happen often, but it did happen. Ben couldn't help but wonder why fate chose him to have two mates. As scared as Audley was of him, he also had to wonder if it was all some cosmic joke.

"It's going to be okay, Audley," Ben said. "You don't have to be afraid anymore. Stefan and I will take good care of you, keep you safe. No one can hurt you anymore."

"You…you don't understand," Audley whispered. "Dane is giving me to Oliver as soon as we get home. I'm going to belong to him."

It was all Ben could do to suppress his growl. Audley belonged to him and Stefan now. Dane and Oliver would never get their hands on the man, not if he had anything to say about it. And he did.

Ben patted Audley's hand, then stood to his feet. He walked over to the phone and picked it up. A moment later he heard Albert answer, just the man he wanted to talk to.

"Albert, it's Ben Nobles," he said. "I'm in the study with Stefan and Audley. We've had a little development here, and I need to see the prince and Devlin, but I don't want anyone else to know. Can you arrange that?"

"Of course, sir," Albert replied. "I'll arrange it immediately."

"You're a gem, Albert."

"Of course, sir."

Ben chuckled as he hung up the phone and turned back to look at Stefan and Audley. "Devlin and Prince Zacarius should be here momentarily. They will help us ensure that Dane and Oliver never get their hands on you again, Audley."

"How?"

Ben walked back over to kneel behind Stefan again. He wrapped his arm around Stefan's shoulder and pulled him back against his larger body. He smiled as he felt Stefan nuzzle the side of his neck and grabbed Stefan's hand and squeezed it to reassure his mate.

"I need to ask you a question, Audley," Ben said, "and I need you to be perfectly honest with me, okay?"

Audley nodded.

"I want you to understand something first. You have three choices here, and Stefan and I will ensure that whichever choice you make, that it's carried out, no matter what anyone says. Understand?"

Audley swallowed, then nodded again.

"Your first choice is to go home with Oliver and Dane." When Audley rapidly shook his head, Ben held up his hand to stop him. "Wait until I'm done, okay?"

Once Audley settled down, Ben continued. "Your second choice is to request asylum from Prince Zacarius," Ben said. "I know he'd give it to you, protect you with his life, as would his mate, Devlin."

"And my third choice?" Audley asked hesitantly.

"Your third choice, Audley," Ben said, "is to have Stefan and I claim you and go home with us as our mate. I know that Prince Zacarius and his royal consort will support whichever decision you make."

"You really want me?" Audley gasped. "Both of you?"

Ben nodded. He felt Stefan's head move against his chest as he nodded, too. "Yes, Audley, we do."

"And you think that the prince will support my decision?"

"I can guarantee it, Audley," Ben replied. "Granted, I don't know much about your prince, but I do know Devlin. We're from the same pack. Devlin would never mate himself to a man he couldn't respect."

"Can I think about it?"

Ben grimaced, but nodded his head anyway. Time was of the essence here. If Audley chose them, Ben wanted to claim the man before anyone could stop him. While he believed the words he told Audley, he'd feel better if he could claim Audley.

"We're going to go over here and give you a few minutes alone, okay?" Ben asked. "But you need to make your decision before Prince Zacarius and Devlin arrive. I know that doesn't give you much time and I'm sorry for that, but it's important, Audley."

Ben climbed to his feet and pulled Stefan up with him. He grabbed Stefan's hand and pulled him over to stand in front of the window, giving Audley privacy to think. Ben hoped he'd make the right choice, but he had just met the man. He had no idea what Audley would decide, but he knew someone who might.

Ben wrapped his arms around Stefan and hugged the smaller man to his chest. He leaned down and rested his chin on top of Stefan's head. Ben just held Stefan for a few moments, savoring the feel of his mate in his arms. No matter what Audley decided, at least he had Stefan.

"Don't worry, my big bad wolf," Stefan whispered against Ben's chest. "Audley will choose us. He just needs to think about it, mull it over in his mind. Audley has never been one to make snap decisions."

"I wish I could be as confident as you, baby, but I have to admit that I'm shaking in my boots here." Ben leaned down and nuzzled the top of Stefan's head. "I don't know what I will do if he denies us."

Stefan tilted his head back and grinned up at Ben. "Trust me, he won't."

Ben chuckled. "Sure of that, are you?"

"How could he possibly resist the two of us?"

"I guess I can't."

Ben jumped and turned to find Audley standing next to them. He hadn't even heard the man walk up. Ben frowned. He must be losing his edge. Either that or his worry clouded everything else.

"Can't what, Audley?" Ben asked softly. The man looked like a stiff wind might blow him over. Ben resolved that if Audley accepted them, he'd get Stefan to cook the man some food and fatten him up a bit.

"I can't resist you," Audley said. "If you still want me, then I choose you and Stefan."

Ben could see the fear in Audley's pale blue eyes. He reached over and held out his hand to Audley. Ben pulled the man in between him and Stefan when he took the hand Ben held out to him. "We still want you, Audley."

"Then how do we do this?"

Ben chuckled. "Well, Stefan and I already started the process when we took your blood. Now you just have to take ours." Ben held his wrist out to Audley. "The rest is up to you."

Audley grabbed Ben's arm and placed his mouth over Ben's wrist. Ben smiled down at him when his pale blue eyes flickered up to his. "Go on, Audley. It's okay."

Elation filled Ben a moment later when Audley's teeth sank into his wrist. The soft pull as Audley suckled the blood from him nearly made Ben's knees give way. Having experienced Stefan's particular brand of biting during sex, Ben couldn't wait to try out his new mate. The mere thought made Ben's cock harden to rock.

Stefan's small gasp caught Ben's attention. He glanced past the erotic sight of Audley licking his wrist to see Stefan's wide, sky-blue eyes. Ben smirked. He knew Stefan could scent his arousal. The smell surrounded them.

Ben also knew that Stefan felt the same arousal. His skin had taken on the warm glow Ben always associated with Stefan being ready for sex. It made Ben feel good to know he wasn't the only one affected by Audley.

"My turn." Stefan groaned as he pushed his wrist in front of Audley's face. Ben chuckled and pulled his own wrist away from Audley. The small bite wound still bled a little. Ben held it out to Stefan, cocking one eyebrow. Stefan leaned in and licked at the wound.

Ben could feel the bond forming between the three of them as Audley bit into Stefan's wrist. It was a heady feeling, almost to the point where Ben felt lightheaded. Not only would he have his wonderful Stefan for the rest of his life, but Audley, the sweetest-looking man he'd ever laid eyes on.

Stefan made Ben burn with desire. He just needed to look at the guy and he wanted to be deep inside of him. Stefan was the type of man who made Ben want to capture him and fuck him into a wall.

Audley was uniquely different. Ben thought he'd met a delicate man when he mated Stefan, but he didn't even come close to being as delicate as Audley looked. Ben would be surprised if the man weighed more than a hundred pounds sopping wet. He looked like a sprite, all fragile and dainty.

Audley made Ben want to cradle the man close to his body and protect him from the evils of the world. He wanted to give the man so much gentle pleasure that he never dreamed there could be anything else. Ben wanted to fulfill all of Audley's fantasies before the man could even realize he had any. He wanted to consume Audley.

Ben couldn't suppress the growl that worked its way up his throat. Exchanging blood wasn't the only part of claiming one's mate. Ben and Stefan needed to claim Audley sexually, too. Ben wanted to finish the claiming right here and now, but the voices coming down the hallway told him he'd run out of time. That part of the claiming would have to wait.

"Close it, Audley," Ben commanded. "Devlin and the prince are coming."

For a moment, Ben saw fire flash in Audley's eyes as the man looked up at him, and then Audley lowered his eyes. Ben groaned at the sight of Audley's small pink tongue swiping against the bite mark on Stefan's wrist. His cock ached and he wondered what else the little man could do with that tongue.

"Is–is it done?" Audley asked, his voice just barely above a whisper.

"It's done, Audley. You belong to Stefan and me now," Ben replied. He gently patted Audley on the shoulder. "No one can take you away from us now—not Oliver, not Dane, not even Prince Zacarius. You're ours."

Audley's smile was tentative, but it was there. That was good enough for Ben. He started to return Audley's smile when the study door opened. Ben stepped in front of Stefan and Audley, protecting his mates from whoever came in. He let out a sigh of relief when he saw Devlin and the prince.

"How's your meeting going?" Ben asked as he let his body settle into a less aggressive mode.

"Oliver's an ass!" Devlin exclaimed.

"I've always thought so." Stefan chuckled, stepping out from behind Ben.

"Dane isn't much better," the prince griped.

"And they're both going to get a lot worse when they find out that Stefan and I just claimed Audley as our mate." Ben held his breath as he waited for the fallout from his words. It wasn't long in coming.

"You did what?" Devlin asked.

"Audley is our mate," Ben said. "Stefan and I have already claimed him. I asked you here so that you could witness our claiming marks. I don't want Oliver or Dane to have any excuse for nullifying our claim."

Ben held out his wrist to Devlin and the prince. Stefan did the same. Ben grabbed Audley's wrist and held his hand out for Devlin and Prince Zacarius to see. The cut he'd received had started to heal, but the evidence still remained in the puckered pink flesh.

"Audley belongs to us and we'll be taking him home with us to Wolf Creek when we leave," Ben said. "Do you have any disagreement with this?"

"You're not going to make this easy for me, are you?" Prince Zacarius asked. He crossed his arms over his chest and glared at Ben.

"Would you deny mates being together?" Ben asked. "We didn't set out to claim Audley, but once we knew he was our mate, we couldn't deny him. Surely you know that?"

Prince Zacarius glanced at Devlin and smiled. "Yes, I'm quite aware of the need to claim your mate."

"Then you won't deny our claim?"

The prince remained quiet for several long, agonizing moments, and then looked past Ben to where Audley huddled behind him. "Audley, how do you feel about all of this? I will give you sanctuary here at the coven estate if you so wish."

Ben was proud of Audley when he stepped forward and shook his head. "No, thank you, your highness. Ben already told me that being here with you and your royal consort was one of my choices. I choose to go with Ben and Stefan."

"Very well," the prince replied. "I will inform Oliver and Dane that Audley has been claimed. You may wish to take your new mate upstairs and complete the claiming before dinner. I have no doubt that Oliver and Dane will pitch a fit if they believe there is any way for them to retain their hold on Audley."

Ben nodded. He'd been thinking along the same lines, but not because of Oliver and Dane. He wanted to complete the claiming so that no one could take Audley away from him and Stefan.

Ben wrapped his arm around Audley's shoulders, then Stefan's, pulling both men into the curve of his body. Ben chuckled and shook his head. The top of Stefan's head barely reached Ben's shoulder. Audley could have fit under his arm. He felt like a giant.

"Come along, my mates," Ben said as he started them all toward the door. "Let's go somewhere more private and get to know each other, hmmm?"

* * * *

Stefan couldn't keep himself from bouncing along as Ben led him and Audley upstairs to their quarters. He was excited. Not only was Ben his, but now Audley, his best friend, was also. Stefan had no idea how he'd become so lucky, but he wasn't about to argue.

He loved Ben, adored the man. He couldn't imagine his life without him. Ben meant everything to him. Audley, though, was Stefan's best friend. They'd played together as children, discovered that they were gay together, everything. Leaving the man behind when he left had been the hardest thing Stefan had ever done.

Stefan did find it a little strange that he never knew he and Audley were mates before now. He couldn't explain it except that maybe they needed Ben to make their little circle complete. Truthfully, he didn't care. He just knew that they were all together now, and that's all that mattered.

The moment Ben opened the door to their room and ushered them in, Stefan grabbed Audley's hand and pulled him over to the bed. He sat down and scooted up on the bed, gesturing for Audley to sit down with him. Ben sat down at the head of the bed, curling around Stefan from behind. It was Stefan's favorite position, being surrounded by Ben like this.

"How have you been, Audley?" Stefan asked. "I mean, really?"

Audley shrugged. "I've been okay, I guess. I missed you, though."

Stefan grabbed Audley's hand and squeezed. "I missed you, too. I wish I could have taken you with me, but once Ben claimed me, you know Oliver would never let me come back. I fully expected Dane to claim me that day."

"Oh, I don't blame you, Stefan," Audley said. Stefan knew it was true. Audley didn't have it in him to stay mad at anyone. "I'm just glad we're back together."

"We are and now we never have to be separated again," Stefan said. He could barely keep his excitement inside. He wanted to laugh, shout, and dance around the room. "You, me, and Ben are finally a family, and no one can separate us."

"I always hoped we'd be together one day," Audley whispered, his face flushing.

Stefan frowned. "You knew we were mates and you never told me? Why not?"

Audley's thin shoulders moved up and down as he shrugged. "There didn't seem to be any point. You know as well as I do that Oliver and Dane would never let us be together and neither of us were strong enough to fight them."

Stefan started laughing. He could feel the confused stares of both his mates. He patted Audley's hand, then reached for Ben's, clasping them both together with his. "I don't think that's going to be a problem anymore, Audley. We have Ben now. He's strong enough for both of us."

"He does look pretty strong," Audley said.

Stefan knew Audley. He knew the look the man gave Ben was one of curiosity. Stefan wanted to increase that curiosity to a fever pitch. Ben was definitely interested. Stefan could smell that in the air. He felt pretty sure the sweet underlying scent was Audley's arousal. Stefan just had to get the two men he wanted together.

He scooted down and leaned back against Ben's wide chest. Audley's eyes widened as Ben's hands came up to wrap around Stefan. Stefan groaned and arched into the fingers that brushed against him. He loved the feeling of Ben's hands on his body.

"Ben is very strong, Audley," Stefan said as he unbuttoned his shirt. "But he has the gentlest hands on earth." Ben's hands moved right in to the opening, his fingers skimming over Stefan's skin. "See?"

Stefan could tell that Audley watched every move of Ben's fingers. His eyes seemed glued to them, following the path they made from Stefan's collarbone down to the waistline of his pants. Stefan sucked in his breath when Ben's fingers pushed under the material of his slacks and brushed against the head of his hard cock.

"Ben," he groaned.

"You like that, baby?" Ben asked.

"God, yes!"

Ben's eyes crinkled as he chuckled. He unbuttoned Stefan's jeans. Stefan lifted his butt up as Ben pushed the pants down his legs. Audley's eyes widened significantly when Stefan's hard cock bounced up and slapped against his abdomen.

Stefan frowned. Audley seemed riveted at the sight of Stefan's cock. That didn't make sense since Stefan knew the man had seen it before. They took baths together as toddlers, skinny dipped as teenagers. They'd even jacked off in the same room a few times. Audley had seen his cock before.

"Audley? Are you okay?"

"Huh?" Audley's head lifted, his dazed eyes meeting Stefan's. "What?"

Stefan chuckled. He leaned forward and rested his hand on Audley's arm. "Are you okay?"

Audley's face flushed. "Yeah, I'm fine."

Stefan patted Audley, then leaned back against Ben's chest. He could feel Ben's amusement in the soft rumble in his chest. It was nice, but Stefan was far more interested in the hard cock that pressed against his back.

Ben reached down and wrapped his hand around Stefan's cock. Stefan moaned and arched his head back into Ben. His mate's touch always felt so good.

"Doesn't this look pretty, Audley?" Ben asked as he shook Stefan's cock in Audley's direction. Audley nodded. "You want to touch it? You can, you know. Stefan is your mate now. You can touch him whenever you want to."

Stefan nearly creamed at the thought of Audley touching him. He held his breath, praying that the man would be bold enough to follow Ben's words. He knew Ben anticipated it as much as he did. Ben's heart thudded in his chest, pounding against Stefan's back.

"I've never—"

"Neither did I before Ben mated me," Stefan said. "But it was more than worth the wait."

Audley's eyes dropped down to Stefan's cock once again. He licked his lips. "Can I—"

"You can do anything you want," Stefan said quickly.

Stefan could see Audley's hand tremble as he reached out and lightly brushed away a small drop of pre-cum from the small slit on the head. Audley's eyes flickered up, then back down as he brought his finger to his mouth and licked the drop away.

Stefan groaned. He heard Ben groan behind him. The sight of Audley licking away proof of Stefan's arousal was intoxicating. It made more drops appear, almost as if they wanted to join the first one.

Stefan shuddered as Audley's hand went back down to his cock. This time, Audley's fingers grazed the top. Ben's hand fell away, only to be replaced by Audley's. Stefan's head fell back against Ben's chest, his eyes fell closed. Audley touched him intimately for the first of what he hoped were many times to come.

"Audley," Stefan cried out. The man's touch was every bit as phenomenal as Ben's. It made Stefan ache with need. His balls felt like they were on fire. He clenched his hands against Ben's jean-clad thighs, then unclenched them.

"Ben," Stefan said, his voice sounding hoarse to even his own ears. "Your pants. Get rid of your pants. I want skin."

"As you desire, my sweet," Ben crooned. He scooted out from behind Stefan and stood beside the bed. Stefan's eyes hated to leave the fascination on Audley's face, but the sight of Ben getting undressed was not one to be missed.

"Audley, watch," Stefan directed, nodding his head toward Ben. Audley's head swung over to Ben. His mouth dropped open as Ben began to strip, one item at a time, slowly. Stefan grinned. Audley's breathing became more rapid with each article of clothing that came off Ben's gorgeous body.

Stefan knew not everyone would find Ben attractive. Many scars marked his body. To Stefan, they had special meaning. He just hoped Audley would see Ben the same way he did. Ben would be crushed if Audley found him hideous.

Stefan was pretty sure it wouldn't be an issue when he heard a small hitch in Audley's breath, but he wasn't positive. The next few seconds would tell the truth. "Gorgeous, isn't he?" Stefan asked.

"So many scars," Audley whispered. "So much pain." Stefan's heart caught at the words. Would Audley reject Ben? Audley's hand reached out to trace one long scar along Ben's abdomen.

Audley looked up at Ben. "Did anyone care for you?"

"Not until Stefan." Ben gave Audley a little smile. "And hopefully you."

Audley looked indecisive. "Why me?" Audley asked. "I mean, I understand Stefan. He's beautiful, but why me? I don't have anything to offer you except a totally insane brother, a man who would trade his own brother to get his hands on me, and the need to feed."

Ben pushed his jeans to the floor, then reached over to caress the side of Audley's face. Audley jumped back, fear clouding his eyes. Ben froze. Audley's face flushed, and he dropped his eyes to look down at his lap.

"I guess that's one thing I have that I can offer you." Audley laughed nervously. "My fear, and I have a lot of it to spare."

Stefan started to lean forward to reassure Audley when Ben knelt on the floor. He slowly reached up to touch Audley's face, giving the man plenty of time to pull away. Stefan knew that Ben wanted to comfort Audley as much as he did, but they'd have to move carefully. Audley looked like a scared rabbit.

"Audley, there's nothing wrong with being afraid," Ben said softly. "Even as big as I am, I get afraid."

Audley snorted in disbelief.

"No, it's true," Ben asserted. "My fears may not be the same as yours, but I do have them."

"What kind of fears?" Audley asked quietly.

Ben gestured to his body. "Look at me. I have scars all over my body, plus I'm the size of a brick shit house. You and Stefan are perfect. You're both small and delicate and don't have a single mark on your bodies. How can I compete with that?"

Audley frowned. "Why would you need to compete?"

Ben chuckled. "There are a lot of more attractive men out there, Audley. What if you or Stefan find someone you want more, someone prettier than me? I worry about that all the time, and the thought of being without either of you scares me to death."

"But we're mates," Audley insisted. "We would never leave you."

"You can't know that. You just met me. You might find you don't even like me once you get to know me."

Audley shook his head. "No, I know Stefan. He's been my best friend since we were babies. If he wants to be with you, then I'll want to be with you. Stefan would never stay with anyone who he didn't care about."

"I love Ben," Stefan said. "I've told him, and even though he says he believes me, I don't think he does." Stefan scooted over to sit next to Audley. His heart filled with joy to be so close to both his mates. "We're just going to have to prove to him that we mean it."

"We?" both Audley and Ben asked.

"Yes, we." Stefan laughed. "I've always had a spot in my heart for Audley and now I know why. We're mates. Now I can love him freely without worrying anyone will think it odd. I know he cares for me as well." Stefan wagged his finger at Ben. "And you, Mr. Nobles, you will hold us together. You're going to be the center that we gravitate around."

Stefan moved closer to slide off the bed, landing on Ben's lap and wrapping his legs around the man's waist. His hands stroked down Ben's chest. "We're going to give you so much love that you won't ever remember living without it."

Stefan leaned up and captured Ben's lips with his own. His tongue swept inside, claiming Ben, trying to tell him without words how much he meant to Stefan. It was urgent and exploratory and made Stefan's heart sing.

When Stefan pulled away, Ben's golden eyes looked glazed. "Audley?" Stefan asked without looking away from Ben. "Would you like to help me show our big guy how we're going to love him?"

Stefan couldn't have been more thrilled when he saw Audley slide down next to him out of the corner of his eyes. Audley's hands joined his on Ben's naked chest. As if by unspoken agreement, Stefan and Audley began caressing Ben, loving on him.

Stefan moved off to the side of Ben. He settled on the floor beside Ben on one side, Audley on the other. Ben groaned. His head fell back on his shoulders and his cock jerked. It was a heady feeling for Stefan to know that he and Audley pleasured Ben so much.

Stefan gestured to Ben's nipples. Both men leaned in at the same time and latched on to the small brown nubs, sucking on them, tugging on them. Stefan immediately felt Ben's hand clench in his hair as the man let out a loud groan. Ben's body shuddered at the twin stimulations.

He glanced over and saw Ben's other hand gripping Audley's hair, but not as tightly. He knew Ben was giving Audley every chance to pull away. Audley didn't look like he had any intention of doing it. He looked happy right where he was.

Stefan stroked his hand down the tight muscles of Ben's abdomen. He grinned around the skin in his mouth at the muscles that rippled under his touch. Ben was so sensitive, so receptive. It was like he was starved for touch. Stefan wanted to give him so much he never felt like he'd been without it.

He trailed his hand down farther, threading his fingers through the thick curly hair at Ben's groin until he could wrap his fingers around the man's hard shaft. He started to stroke his hand down Ben's length when he felt another hand grip Ben right next to him.

Stefan glanced down, excitement building in him when he saw Audley's hand right next to his. He started stroking, noting that Audley's rhythm was a little unsteady, but after a moment, the smaller man was moving right along with him.

Ben seemed to be enjoying it. The thick muscles on Ben's thighs bunched and trembled as he thrust himself forward into Stefan and Audley's hands. Stefan could feel the barely controlled restraint in his motions. The man was on the edge.

If it had been just the two of them, Stefan had no doubt that he would have either been on his hands and knees with a cock in his ass by now or flat on his back. With Audley there, Ben was trying hard, fighting with himself, to not scare their new mate.

Stefan wanted Ben and Audley to both experience how wonderful he believed it could be between the three of them if they could all just learn to trust in each other. He needed to do that. He needed to bring his best friend and his lover together.

Stefan released his grip on Ben's cock and moved it down farther to cup Ben's balls in his hand, massaging them gently between his fingers. He let Audley have Ben's full length and that was a lot of inches to have for anyone, especially someone of Audley's size.

"Stefan," Ben groaned. "Give me your ass."

Excitement made Stefan's heart pound faster. He could hear the need in Ben's deep rumble. He let go of Ben's nipple and reached over to the small bottle on the nightstand. Popping the top, he squirted a fair amount on Ben's fingers, then turned around and presented his ass to the man.

Resting on his hands and knees, Stefan could see Audley's hard cock bouncing right in front of him. It was too much of a temptation to miss. He scooted up a bit and licked across the glistening head. His reward was the low moan from Audley and the shaking of his entire body. It was wonderful.

Stefan did it again, then butted at Audley's abdomen until the man turned toward him slightly and spread his knees, opening himself up to Stefan's questing mouth. Stefan immediately sank down on Audley's entire length, swallowing until he felt the head of Audley's cock hit the back of his throat.

"Sweet hell, Stefan," Ben moaned. "That is so fucking hot. Swallow that cock. Show Audley how perfect your mouth is."

Stefan groaned. His eyes rolled back in his head as lust ignited in his body. Ben knew how much Stefan liked to hear him talk dirty. He knew what a turn on it was for Stefan. That, combined with the fingers in his ass nearly made Stefan come right then, but he wanted to feel Ben deep in his ass when he did.

Stefan pulled his mouth off of Audley's cock long enough to glance over at Ben, pleading. "Ben, please."

Ben grinned. He pulled his fingers free and smacked Stefan on the ass. "Grab the lube and get Audley ready. You can have his ass while I have yours."

Stefan's eyes snapped up to Audley's. "Is that okay with you, Audley?"

Audley flushed, but nodded his head. Stefan smiled and motioned with his hand for Audley to turn around. Audley started to turn around, then paused, frowning as he glanced over his shoulder at Stefan.

"Can't we look at each other while we do this?" Audley asked. "Do I have to be facing away from you?"

"Of course we can look at each other," Stefan quickly replied, "but it might be easier for you on your hands and knees the first time."

Audley shook his head, looking hesitant and a bit anxious. "I'd rather be able to see you."

"Then let's climb up on the bed," Stefan said.

The climb up onto the bed was quickly accomplished. Audley scooted back to lie back on the pillows at the top of the bed, Stefan knelt between his spread legs, and Ben behind him. Stefan's hands trembled as he squirted lube out onto his fingers.

He was excited. The hands playing with his ass didn't help. They drove him crazy, moving over his ass, between his cheeks, and down to massage his balls. It was all Stefan could do to move gently with Audley. But he soon had the man squirming and whimpering, pressing back against the fingers Stefan thrust into his tight hole.

"Are you about ready for Stefan, Audley?" Ben asked. His voice didn't sound quite steady. "I'm not going to be able to hold out much longer."

Audley nodded rapidly.

Stefan moved up and started to fit the head of his cock to Audley's pink entrance when a thought suddenly hit him. He leaned up farther and kissed Audley deeply. When he lifted his lips, he looked into the pale-green eyes blinking back at him.

"Is this what you want, Audley?" he whispered.

Audley smiled and nodded his head. Stefan leaned into the hand Audley cupped around his cheek, his eyes almost falling closed at the tender gesture. "I've wanted this since I first recognized we were mates. I just never thought it would happen." Audley's eyes moved past Stefan to encompass Ben. "Or that I'd have Ben, too."

That was good enough for Stefan. Not only did it answer his question, but it sent his heart pounding and made the breath catch in his throat. Stefan blinked several times, telling himself that he was just reacting to the dust in the air…really.

He grabbed Audley's legs and looped them over his arms, then pressed forward with his cock. His eyes started to water again as he watched his cock sink into Audley for the very first time. They fit together so perfectly.

The moment was made even more perfect when Ben sank into him from behind. Stefan's fingers dug into Audley's hips when Ben bottomed out, his body pressing against Stefan's. For a moment, everyone froze, caught up in the moment, their first time connected all together. It was a time that would never happen again. It was special.

"If you don't fucking move I'm going to scream!"

Stefan's eyes snapped down to Audley, his jaw dropping at the fierce look on the man's face. He had never heard Audley speak like this. Audley was the quiet, shy one, the reserved one. He never demanded something and he never swore.

"Audley?"

"Please, Stefan." Audley whimpered, a quick change from his demanding words a moment before. "I can't stand it. I ache. I need—I need—"

"I have you, Audley," Stefan said as he started to move, thrusting slowly into him.

"And I have you both." Ben growled in his ear. "You feel that, baby. I'm fucking both of you."

Stefan could barely keep from melting into a pile of goo when Ben moved in him. The power behind Ben's thrust shoved Stefan into Audley. When Ben pulled back, so did Stefan. Ben really did have them both.

"Next time, Audley gets to be in the middle," Ben said. "You'd like that, wouldn't you, Audley? Wouldn't you like to fuck Stefan while I fuck your tight little ass?"

Stefan cried out when Audley's inner muscles suddenly tightened down around his cock like a vice, white spunk shooting between them as Audley came. He almost closed his eyes at the exquisite feeling, but the vision below him won out. Audley's head was arched back, his eyes closed, and his mouth slightly open as he groaned. He looked stunning.

The corded muscles on Audley's arched neck drew Stefan's attention. He licked his lips as he watched the small pulse thump in his throat. He could feel his fangs drop down, anticipating the taste of his mate.

Stefan could feel his orgasms cresting, his body ready to explode. He leaned down and sank his teeth into Audley's throat. The sweet taste of Audley's life-giving blood flooded his mouth and overloaded his senses.

He felt Ben's canines bite into his shoulder, and that was all Stefan needed to send him over the edge. His loud roar of completion matched Ben's, both men coming at the same time. Stefan filled Audley with his seed as Ben filled him, the simultaneous stimulations almost more than Stefan could handle.

Stefan's vision dimmed. His head reeled. He had just enough forethought to pull his fangs free from Audley's throat before he collapsed down on the man, his head resting on Audley's shoulder.

He felt soft, delicate hands rub his back as he tried to catch his breath. It wasn't easy, especially when Ben's knot extended and took hold inside of him, connecting them together. A small part of Stefan mourned the fact that he didn't have a similar way to connect him to Audley.

"What's wrong, baby?" Ben asked softly as he hugged Stefan's back. "You should be happy right now. We've claimed Audley. No one can ever take him from us again."

"I am," Stefan said. "I just wish—I wish that I was a werewolf like you so that I could knot Audley," Stefan said. "I wish that we were all connected together."

"Stefan, what you and Audley give us is way better than any knot," Ben said as he rubbed his hand up and down Stefan's arm.

"Remember that life thread thing you told me about? You and Audley will give us a lot more years together, years we wouldn't have if we were all werewolves."

"I guess," Stefan said, not entirely convinced. He sighed and tilted his head up when Ben snuggled into his neck.

"I know so, Stefan," Ben murmured against his skin.

"I have a question," Audley said quietly.

Stefan looked down at the man wrapped in his arms. "Yeah?"

"What's a knot?"

Chapter 6

Audley peeked past Stefan's astonished face to Ben's, smiling when he saw the amused look he had. He wasn't sure what was acceptable to ask and what wasn't. He didn't want to step out of line or cross any boundaries he wasn't supposed to.

"I'm a shifter, Audley," Ben said. "My human side and my werewolf side coexist together, and when I find my mate and make love to him, I knot him."

"I get that part, but what is a knot?" Audley asked.

"A knot is a small extension at the end of my cock. When I ejaculate, it extends and takes a hold inside of my mate so that we're basically connected together for a while after we have sex."

"Does it hurt?"

Audley was surprised when Stefan's face flushed and he chuckled. "No, not exactly," he said. "It actually feels pretty good."

"Will you knot me if we have sex?"

"You're my mate just as much as Stefan is, Audley," Ben said. "So, I imagine I will."

"Can I see it?"

Ben started laughing, Stefan too. Audley dropped his head, his face flushed red with mortification. He knew he shouldn't have asked, but his curiosity overrode that knowledge. Audley tried to bury his face in the pillows.

"Audley?" Stefan said softly. "Audley, look at me, please."

Audley shook his head, too embarrassed to lift it.

"Ben, do something," Stefan demanded. "Audley is—damn! I hate that part."

Once again, Audley's curiosity got the better of him and he lifted his head just in time to see Ben reach over Stefan for him. A small squeak escaped his lips and he shut his eyes as Ben lifted him up over Stefan and settled him between the two men.

"Open your eyes, Audley."

Audley slowly opened his eyes to find Ben leaning directly over him. It was only as Ben's hand moved to caress his face that he realized their naked bodies were pressed together. Stefan pressed against his back.

"Now you listen to me, Audley," Ben said. "The only stupid question is the one you don't ask. If you want to know something, if you need something—hell, if you just want something—I expect you to ask. Understand?"

Audley nodded, too stunned to answer verbally.

"The reason Stefan and I were laughing is because the only time the knot comes out is after I'm already inside of you. I've never even seen it."

"Oh."

"Yeah…oh." Stefan laughed.

Ben rolled over on top of Audley, arching an eyebrow at him. "I'd be happy to show you the knot."

Audley giggled. Ben was grinning, his eyebrows moving up and down as he wiggled them. The look on his face was clearly a lecherous one. The cock growing hard against Audley's abdomen was a pretty good indication of Ben's intentions, too.

Audley opened his mouth to reply to Ben when the bedroom door flew open. Before Audley could even see who it was, Ben rolled him and Stefan off the opposite side to the floor. They landed with a painful thud, Ben crouching over the top of them. A low, threatening growl filled the room.

"Where is he?" someone shouted. "Where is the little shit?"

Audley peered over the side of the bed. He gasped, a shiver of panic shooting through him when he spotted Dane and Oliver standing just inside of the room. The rage blossoming in their faces didn't bode well for any of them.

"Audley, you little shit," Dane shouted as he looked wildly around the room. "I know you're in here. If you don't come out right now I'm going to kick the shit out of you before I give you to Oliver."

"Get out, now!" Ben shouted as he jumped to his feet. Audley watched as the gentle man who had just made love to him and Stefan started to shift. Ben's hands turned into claws, and his mouth turned almost into a muzzle, his teeth scaring the shit out of Audley.

"This doesn't concern you, dog," Dane snarled. "We're here for our mates."

"My mates," Ben growled, his voice distorted from his huge teeth. "I've claimed them, you can't have them. But you can have your lives if you leave now and never come near them again."

"There's two of us and only one of you, shifter." Oliver snickered. "You're fucking nuts if you think you can take us both."

"Last chance," Ben sneered. "Are you going to do the smart thing and leave?"

Instead of answering, Dane and Oliver exchanged a sly look, then launched themselves at Ben. Audley was stunned to see how quickly Ben moved. He was magnificent, all lean muscle and powerful strength moving in one fluid motion.

Before Dane could even hit Ben with the fist he had raised, Ben scraped huge claw marks up Dane's chest to his throat. Unfortunately, that left Oliver the opening he needed to jump on Ben's back and sink in his fangs.

"Don't hurt him," Stefan yelled, racing over to the nightstand to grab a lamp. Ben frantically clawed at Oliver on his back before he could drain him dry. Stefan jumped from the side of the bed to where they were fighting in the middle of the room. He brought the lamp over his head and smacked Oliver with it so hard the lamp shattered.

"Come here, you little fuck," Dane roared, grabbing Stefan. They were at a disadvantage with how quickly vampires healed. "Where's Audley?"

"He's not here," Stefan lied, getting a backhand from Dane that sent him flying. Audley wanted to help, he screamed inside to make his body move. It just wouldn't listen. Dane was on Stefan the second he landed on the floor. Audley watched, paralyzed, as Dane sank his fangs into Stefan trying to weaken him.

At the same time, Ben took the opportunity Stefan created with Oliver. Ripping him off his back, Ben sank his large teeth into Oliver's neck. Oliver fought, clawing every inch of Ben he could reach. Audley finally had an idea. He scooted his butt back closer to the head of the bed. Without taking his eyes off the fight, he reached up and grabbed the phone.

"Hello?" Albert said from the other end of the phone.

"Help, Albert," Audley whispered, crying. "Oliver and Dane found us in Ben's room. They're trying to kill Ben and Stefan. I can't help them."

"Hang tight, sir," Albert replied quickly. "I'll send help immediately."

Audley didn't even get the chance to say thank you, as Albert started yelling out to people on the other side of the phone. He just hoped his mates could hang on until help arrived. He glanced back over to the fight in front of him. It looked like Stefan was being drained. Audley sucked up what courage he could find. He'd rather die than let his mates die.

Seeing the poker in the fireplace, Audley ran over and grabbed it. Before he lost his nerve, Audley jumped and slammed the poker into Dane's side as hard as he could. Audley quickly dropped to the ground, just missing Dane's claws aimed for him.

He saw Oliver making a mess of Ben's back, long claws raking across naked skin. Audley knew his mate couldn't take much more. As it stood, Ben didn't have any skin left on his back that wasn't injured. But still, his wolf wouldn't let up his hold on Oliver's neck, tearing into it as much as he could.

Audley searched around for another weapon, anything he could use to defend his mates. He spotted a pocket knife sticking out of the pocket of Ben's pants.

He grabbed it and launched himself at Oliver's back, sinking it in as deep as he could where Oliver's heart should have been. That is, if Oliver actually had a heart. He wasn't as quick this time and Oliver's clawed hand reached around and ripped into Audley. He tried to ignore the intense pain flaring through his face.

"I'm going to kill you for this, brother," Dane growled as he reached Audley, ripping him off Oliver and throwing him to the floor. His face was bleeding too badly to open his eyes, but Audley knew the voice of his brother all too well.

He felt claws rake across his chest, just as the other voices started shouting in the room. Suddenly Dane wasn't on top of him anymore. "He's my brother. I have a right to end his life," Dane shouted.

"Not in my coven, you don't," he heard Prince Zacarius shout back. "My word is law here. You knew I gave my blessing to this mating."

"Vampires can't mate with shifters," Oliver screamed. "We already promised our brothers to each other. Even you can't go against that, Prince."

"Yes, he can," Audley heard Devlin yell. "And nothing overrules the mating bond. Ben is mated to Stefan and Audley. We told you this. Your prince gave his decree, and you ignored it."

"Stefan, I can't see," Audley cried out. "Are you and Ben okay?"

"Stefan's unconscious, little one," Devlin said softly, picking him up. Audley felt the mattress under him a moment later. He blushed when he realized he was still all naked, but someone pulled a blanked over him just then.

"Ben is hurt pretty bad, Audley," Devlin continued, "but it shouldn't be life threatening."

"Stefan can only drink from me or Ben," Audley cried out. "He can have all the blood from me he needs. I just can't see him to feed him. Can you bring him to me?"

The mattress beside Audley dipped, and he felt a warm body press against his side. Audley reached out and mapped the body next to him, instantly knowing that it was Stefan by the size of the arms and legs he touched.

"Where's Ben?" he asked frantically. He couldn't see much of anything. Lights flashed before his eyes and his head swam every time he turned it. Audley knew he'd heal, but an injury this severe would take time.

"I'm right here, baby," Ben said as the mattress on the other side of Audley dipped with the larger man's weight. Audley reached out for him, hearing a small hiss of pain when his hand connected with Ben's injured chest. "Careful, baby, these are going to take a little while to heal up."

"Wha–what happened?" Audley asked. "Where's Dane and Oliver?"

"Not to worry, Audley," Ben said. "Prince Zacarius and his men took them away. I imagine that your prince is plenty pissed off that they ignored his directive. Oliver and Dane are in a lot of trouble right now."

"Good!"

Ben chuckled and wrapped an arm around Audley, pulling him close. "How are you feeling, baby? Any lasting pain?" Audley felt Ben's gentle fingers probe around his eyes. "Does this hurt?"

Audley nodded, but the protective mating scent coming from Ben's body filled the air around him. He turned his head toward the strong scent and inhaled deeply. Almost instantly, relief and a feeling of security filled him. Overwhelmed, Audley whimpered.

"Shh, baby," Ben whispered against his hair. His strong arms tightened around Audley's body. "I have you. I know I failed to keep you safe this time, but I swear I will never let it happen again."

"No, no," Audley said, shaking his head rapidly. "You didn't do this. Oliver and Dane did. You did everything you could to keep me and Stefan safe." Audley paused for a moment, resting his head against Ben's shoulder. "No one's ever tried to keep me safe before."

"I will always keep you safe, Audley," Ben murmured. "You belong to me now, me and Stefan. No one gets to hurt you anymore. No one gets to touch you anymore, not if you don't want it."

"Does that include you and Stefan?" Audley asked. He was basically just curious. He didn't mean for Ben to drop his arms and move away from him.

"Of course it does, Audley," Ben said quietly. His voice sounded even, calm, but the tension in his body belied that stillness. "You have the right to say whenever anyone touches you, even me or Stefan."

"Do I have the right to ask you to touch me?" Audley's voice was barely above a whisper as he asked for the one thing he never asked anyone. He was afraid of Ben's answer, be it acceptance or rejection. Both scared him.

"Always," Ben said.

"Then would—" Audley swallowed, his throat feeling as dry as the Sahara. "Would you hold me again?" Audley asked.

Ben's arms instantly surrounded him again. This time, despite the healing wounds on Ben's chest, Audley was pulled tight against his mate. "I'll always hold you when you want me to, Audley."

Audley could feel tears prickle the corner of his eyes. He squeezed the man tight and buried his face in Ben's neck. The strong masculine scent that was so much a natural part of his mate filled Audley's senses.

"Please don't ever let me go," he whispered, suddenly afraid that this was all a dream. He didn't know if he could handle it if all of this was suddenly taken away from him.

Ben's hand rubbed Audley's back, moving down to curb around the rounded globe of his ass, pulling Audley even closer. Audley lifted his leg and hooked it over Ben's hip. He could feel his body press close to his mate, their cocks coming to life as they mashed together.

"Never, baby," Ben promised. "You're mine now, and I'm never going to let you go."

Audley closed his eyes and leaned his head against Ben again, inhaling his deep scent. He felt like he was wrapped in a silken cocoon of euphoria. Ben wanted him, Stefan wanted him. And Oliver would never have him.

"Ben? Audley?" Stefan called out, his voice rough with anxiety.

Audley quickly turned over and reached for the man he knew lay next to him. His vision was getting better, but it was not all of the way healed. He could see shapes in shades of gray, blurred motions.

"Stefan?"

"Audley, are you okay?"

"I will be," Audley replied. He started feeling over Stefan's body, searching for injuries. "I can't see very well, but it's getting better. What about you? The royal consort said you were unconscious."

"I'm okay," Stefan replied. "I need—I need to—"

Audley smiled. "You need to feed," he said. Sudden elation filled him when he realized that he could give back to his mate for all of the things Stefan gave him throughout the years. He scooted closer and tilted his head back, feeling it lay against Ben's shoulder. "Take what you need, Stefan."

"But you are injured, Audley," Stefan protested. "I can't—"

"Please, let me do this for you." Audley knew that there was an edge to his voice, a desperate pleading. He needed to do this for Stefan, and Ben, too. He needed to be able to give back to both of them.

"All right, Audley," Stefan finally said, "but you tell me if I take too much."

Audley nodded. A moment later, he felt Stefan lean toward him. A wet tongue swiped over his throat right where his pulse beat so rapidly. It felt hot, made him feel achy. His hands trembled and he clenched them against Stefan's naked shoulders as he felt the man's fangs sink into his neck.

"Stefan," he whispered in a velvet murmur. Each pull of Stefan's mouth on his skin felt like a pull on his cock. Before he knew it, Audley was pumping his hips against Stefan. Audley's face burned. He was mortified by his reaction, but he couldn't seem to stop. It felt too good.

"God, baby, that is so fucking hot," Ben groaned in his ear. Audley's breath hitched in his throat when he felt Ben's hand trail down between his ass cheeks to press against his sensitive hole. "Can I have you, Audley? Can I take you, baby?"

Audley started to nod, but quickly remembered the fangs deep in his throat. Instead, he lifted his leg and pulled it up to his chest, letting his calf rest over Stefan's hip. His gesture seemed to be enough for Ben. The man sank his fingers into Audley's stretched entrance, three of them at once.

Audley groaned, the twin sensations of Stefan at his neck and Ben at his ass fueling the fire starting in his body. He felt the head of Ben's cock nudge his puckered entrance, his body shuddering in anticipation.

Audley reached back and grabbed Ben's hip, digging his fingers into the man's skin as he tried to pull him closer. He needed to feel his mate take him. He needed to know Ben was okay just as much as he did Stefan.

In giving Ben his body and Stefan his blood, he was providing for both of them. He was taking care of both of his mates. That knowledge was more powerful than any orgasm he ever experienced.

Still, the feeling of Ben's thick cock sinking into his ass as Stefan continued to drink his life-giving blood was something Audley promised himself he would repeat as many times as his mates let him.

Ben started moving, his hips thrusting forward, impaling Audley on the man's rather impressive cock. Audley reached down and wrapped his hands around his and Stefan's cocks, stroking them together. He grinned when he heard a low groan come from Stefan, and the man started moving with him.

This is it, Audley thought to himself. *This is why I was created.*

His heart sang with delight from each groan that came from Ben and Stefan. His heart jolted and his pulse pounded as something intense flared between the three of them, a connection that bonded them together for all time.

A delicious shudder heated his body. The flames burning through him grew higher, hotter. Audley started panting. He could feel Ben's cock open him up every time the man thrust forward, awakening nerve endings that were dormant until today. Stefan discovered them, Ben exploited them. Audley just laid there and eagerly accepted it.

The tugs he gave his and Stefan's cock became erratic as his mind lost connection with reality and moved into a red haze dominated by only the three of them. Stefan pressed against Audley's front, Ben at his back. Audley was totally encircled by both of his mates.

The heat was tremendous—overwhelming—and Audley jumped into it with both feet. He cried out as ropes of pearly white spunk shot between him and Stefan. As Stefan pulled his fangs free and arched, crying out his own release, Audley was overcome by a need to taste the man. He struck at the arched neck in front of him, his sharp fangs easily sinking into Stefan's soft flesh.

White-hot, sweet blood flooded his mouth. An ache grew in Audley as the dormant sexuality of his body awakened. His breath came in long, surrendering moans. He felt Ben's hands tighten around him. Ben's cock throbbed and swelled inside of Audley. Then Ben roared, filling Audley with his release.

A moan of ecstasy escaped Audley's lips as the knot in Ben's cock extended and took hold inside his body. Audley realized that up until that second, he never truly believed he was mated to Ben, that he would be able to keep the man forever. It felt too much like a dream. But if what Ben and Stefan said was true, Ben would only knot his mates and that was Stefan and Audley.

Audley knew he was mated to Stefan. He'd known for years that they were mates, ever since they hit puberty and Stefan's scent changed. It had drawn him, attracted him, made him realize what he wanted in life. Audley just never thought he'd get it.

Now he had both. Audley's heart nearly burst with overwhelming feelings of love and relief, draining away all of his doubts. He had been claimed by both of his mates, a claiming that would be recognized in both vampire and werewolf worlds.

Chapter 7

Ben knew something was wrong before he even opened his eyes to look around. Stefan was snuggled up to him on one side. Audley should have been snuggled up to him on the other side, but the spot was empty.

Panic slammed into Ben instantly. He rolled to the side of the bed as carefully as he could, not wanting to wake Stefan unless he needed to. Ben grabbed his pajama bottoms off the floor and pulled them up his legs, standing up.

Lifting his nose to the air, Ben sniffed for Audley's unique scent. He was able to hone in on the sweet fragrance almost immediately. No one smelled quite like Audley. At the moment, Ben was eternally grateful for that.

Ben followed his nose downstairs to the dining room. He paused in the doorway, his heart rate returning to normal when he found Audley sitting in a chair, bent over something in his hands.

He seemed intent on whatever he was doing, humming softly to himself. Ben could just see the glint of steel moving between Audley's hands. He figured Audley must be working with some sort of knife, so he moved carefully when he stepped over to the table and into Audley's view.

"What do you have there, Audley?" he asked as he sat down next to Audley. As softly as he spoke, Audley still jumped, nicking his thumb with the knife in his hand.

"Crap!" Audley cried out before lifting his hand to his mouth. Ben caught Audley's wrist before he could lick the blood off, bringing the injured digit to his own mouth. Sweet, hot blood rushed across his tongue.

He glanced up at Audley through his eyelashes. The man seemed mesmerized by the sight of his finger in Ben's mouth. He licked his lips as he intently watched Ben lick the blood away.

"Delicious," Ben murmured.

Audley's pale-green eyes flickered up to meet Ben's. His lower lip caught between his teeth. Ben wasn't sure he'd ever seen anything so sexy. Audley had gorgeous, delicate looks, much like Stefan, but he had one thing Stefan didn't have...innocence.

Ben had no doubt after the last two weeks of being mated to the man that Audley wasn't innocent, but there was this air of naïveté about Audley that made him adorable and totally irresistible.

Ben wanted to wrap him in cotton wool and protect him from the world. He wanted to be Audley's hero. He also wanted to fuck the man into the wall and mess up his pure little world. The need to debauch the man was almost overwhelming.

He started to pull Audley toward him when he noticed the small wooden piece in his mate's hand. He frowned, his eyebrows drawing together as he reached for the object. "What is this, baby?"

Audley's face flushed red. He immediately tried to pull the wooden piece away, hiding it behind his back. "Nothing," Audley whispered.

Ben just held his hand out until Audley slowly brought the object back from behind his back and laid it in Ben's open palm. Ben turned it over and over, marveling at the craftsmanship of the wood carving. It was exquisite.

Carved into a single piece of wood was a perfect cast of Ben holding Stefan and Audley in his arms, all of them naked. He knelt on the ground, Stefan straddling one of his thighs and Audley the other. His head was arched back, a look of pure bliss on his face as Stefan and Audley drank from his neck.

"Audley," he whispered. "This is... this is..." He glanced at Audley's cautious face. "This is the most beautiful thing I've ever seen. You did this?"

Audley nodded, a small smile starting to cross his lips. "I wanted to make you something," Audley whispered. He glanced down at the tabletop, twisting his fingers together nervously. "Stefan does so much. He cooks and cleans and helps you get ready for work."

Audley shrugged. "I just wanted to make you something to show you—I can't do those things and—" Audley's face flushed again and he dropped his eyes even more, staring down at his lap. "I know it was stupid but—"

Ben set the carving down on the table and reached over to lift Audley onto his lap. He brushed Audley's white-blond hair back from his face and tilted his chin up. "Look at me, baby."

Audley was slow to raise his eyes. When he did, Ben inhaled deeply at the uncertainty blazing in them. One of these days, when Audley felt more comfortable in their relationship, Ben wanted to know the horrible things that had happened to his mate before they were together. Someone had abused Audley so much that he doubted his own worth.

Ben needed to put a stop to that. He needed to make Audley know how much he was wanted, needed, how much Audley was loved. Ben tucked Audley's head under his chin and wrapped his arms around him.

"I want you to listen to me very carefully, Audley, okay?"

Audley nodded after a moment. Ben grimaced at his hesitation. He tamped down on his feelings of anger at what had been done to Audley, promising to himself that he would give Audley more love and caring than the man could stand.

"I don't know much about love," he began. "I never learned. I knew from the time I hit puberty that I would be a soldier in our pack. That's what I was made for. Because of that, I didn't make a lot of friends. I never wanted to have to fight someone I cared about."

"I don't want you to fight at all."

"I don't like fighting either, Audley, but someone has to do it. I'm a big guy, where most of our pack isn't. I'm also very good at what I do. I've trained a lot for it."

Audley tilted his head back and carefully traced the long scar running from the corner of Ben's right eye down his cheek to the bottom of his jaw. "But you've paid such a high price for it," he whispered. "And you never had anyone to take care of you, to love you. That isn't how it should be."

Audley's heart was so big and giving that it almost brought tears to Ben's eyes. He had to blink several times just to keep that from happening. "I have you and Stefan now, though, and that makes everything I've done in the past, everything I do now, worth anything I go through."

Audley's brows drew together in an agonized expression. "Do you really believe that?"

"I do, Audley," Ben said. "You two give me more than I could ever have imagined having in my life."

"Even me?" Audley asked. "I mean, I understand Stefan. He's wonderful. He's beautiful to look at and he shows his caring in everything he does. But I–I can't even cook."

"Audley, I never asked you to cook," Ben said. He picked up the wood carving and held it out in front of Audley. "Besides, Stefan can't carve like this. Neither can I. Between the three of us, only you can create something so beautiful."

"You think it's beautiful?"

"Yes, but nearly as beautiful as you are," Ben said as he fingered a loose tendril of hair on Audley's cheek. "I think you've created something wonderful and I love it, but it doesn't hold a candle to you."

"Me?" Audley's fingers fluttered at his neck.

Ben chuckled. "Yes, Audley. You."

"But what about Stefan?"

"What about him?"

"Don't you—isn't he—he's just so—"

Leaning down, Ben slowly curled his hand in Audley's hair and pulled his head back. He wanted to see his mate's pale-green eyes when he spoke. He wanted Audley to see the truth in his eyes.

"Stefan is everything to me," Ben began. "He loved me despite how I looked, how much of a beast I am. He saw something in me that I didn't even know that I had. However, that doesn't discount what you've given me, Audley."

"Me?" Audley asked again, his voice almost a squeak.

"You are a ray of sunshine in my darkness, Audley," Ben said. "Stefan showed me there was light in the world. You brighten it so I can see all the beauty around me. I don't think I could survive now without either of you."

"Well, yeah. We're your mates."

"Yes, you and Stefan are my mates, but it's more than that, Audley," Ben said. He wished there was an easier way to explain the feelings he had for both Audley and Stefan, but he was never very good with explanations. He never told Stefan of his love because he didn't know how to put his feelings into words. Ben suddenly realized that while Stefan might understand his hesitation, Audley needed to hear the actually words to believe. "Being mated doesn't mean we have to care about each other. I've known mates who couldn't stand each other. Mating just draws us together. The rest is all up to us."

"What's that mean?" Audley frowned.

Ben picked Audley up and swung him around until the man straddled his thighs, facing him. He cupped Audley's face in his hands. "It means that even though it's not required for a mating, I need you and Stefan more than the air I breathe. I can't live without either one of you."

Ben saw more than heard the soft hitch in Audley's breathing. His eyes widened, his slender hands unconsciously twisted together. "You love me?" Audley whispered so softly that if Ben hadn't been watching Audley's face so intently, he never would have known the man spoke.

"Yes, Audley. I love you."

Audley's eyes watered, one small tear falling down his porcelain-colored cheek. "No one's ever loved me."

"I think Stefan has always loved you," Ben said. "I just think he didn't recognize what that was because of the situation you both lived in. Now that you're both here, he's finally been freed to love you the way he's always wanted to."

"And that doesn't bother you?"

"Why should it?" Ben asked. "Just because Stefan loves you doesn't mean he can't love me. In fact, I think it gives him even more reason to love us both. We both bring something different to our relationship."

Ben smiled at Audley's confused face and reached for the wooden statue the man carved. "You made this because you wanted to give me something to show me how much you cared for me, right?"

Audley flushed, but nodded.

"Stefan can't carve an apple to save his life, but he does make a fabulous apple pie. Both things show caring, but both are different. Just like you and Stefan. You both care for me. You just show it in different ways."

"You know that I—that I—"

"You show me you care every time you let me hold your hand, Audley, every time you let me touch your face," Ben said as he caressed the side of Audley's face. He set the carving down on the table and reached for Audley, pulling him up close until their noses nearly touched. "You show me that you care every time you let me love you."

Ben leaned in just enough to feel Audley's breath blow across his face, letting his tongue brush over the man's lush lips. He could feel the nervous clenching and unclenching of Audley's hands against his bare shoulders.

His hand slid down Audley's hips and tightened around his ass. He lifted the smaller man against him, pressing their bodies together. The hard cock trapped in his pajama bottoms would leave no doubt how Ben felt about Audley, how much he was turned on by the other man.

Ben groaned as Audley's hands moved off his shoulders to grip his hair, pulling Ben's mouth closer and mashing their lips together. He pulled Audley's shirt up to his armpits, then slid his hands under the waistband of his pajama bottoms, cupping the man's perfect little ass in his hands.

Ben totally approved when Audley broke their kiss and leaned back to whip his shirt over his head, tossing it over his shoulder. He was back instantly, pressing his lips against Ben's again. Ben could feel Audley's svelte, hairless chest move against his, and it made his toes curl.

"More," Audley moaned in his ears.

Ben was more than happy to comply with Audley's demand. He lifted Audley up with one hand and ripped his pajama bottoms away with the other. He then pushed his own pajama bottoms down to his feet, kicking them away. When their bodies met as Ben set Audley on his lap, Ben felt Audley tremble.

He hoped it was a good tremble. From the small whimpers coming from Audley and the way he pushed down against Ben's hard cock, Ben was pretty sure Audley enjoyed himself. He wanted Audley to more than enjoy himself. He wanted Audley to lose his mind.

"We need some sort of lube, baby," Ben reminded Audley.

Audley didn't lift his head from kissing along Ben's jaw line. He just pointed to the kitchen. Ben chuckled and stood to his feet, wrapping his hands under Audley's ass as he lifted the man in his arms and walked into the kitchen.

When Ben turned his head away from Audley to search through the pantry shelves, Audley just latched into his neck. He nibbled and sucked, scraping his fangs across Ben's skin. It was a tease because he never quite broke the skin, but it sent shivers of delight down Ben's body.

Ben had to stop searching several times when the sensations burning through his body became too much. Here he wanted to be the one that drove Audley out of his mind and he was about to come right where he stood. Despite what the man thought, Audley was very good at what he did. And what he did was drive Ben crazy.

He quickly searched the rest of the cupboards until he found a bottle of cooking oil. He grimaced and then decided it would do in a pinch when he felt Audley's hips begin to undulate against his.

Unscrewing the lid, he poured some out on his hands, then set the bottle on the counter. Lifting Audley with one hand, Ben pushed his other one between Audley's butt cheeks, searching for the tight little hole he knew waited for him.

Audley's passionate moan as Ben pushed one finger into it rang in Ben's ears. It made him feel like he had won the lottery. It made him feel so aroused that his vision shimmered at the edges, and his breath caught in his throat.

Ben quickly pushed another finger into Audley's tight hole, needing to stretch the man out swiftly before he embarrassed himself by ejaculating all over the floor like an untried teenage boy. It was still going to be close.

Ben laid Audley back down on the tabletop and pushed a third finger into Audley. The green eyes staring back up at him with a dazed look was the biggest aphrodisiac Ben could ever remember experiencing. But it was nothing compared to the lust that ripped through him when Audley grinned and let his legs fall apart, baring everything to Ben's hungry eyes.

"Damn, Audley," Ben groaned. "You're so fucking perfect."

Audley held his arms out, reaching for Ben. "Need you."

Ben pulled his fingers free and grabbed for the bottle of oil. He quickly poured more on his cock, spilling several drops on the floor in his haste. Setting the bottle on the table, he grabbed his cock and pushed it against Audley's puckered hole, watching as he slowly sank into the man's tight grip.

"Sweet hell, Audley," he groaned. His mate's body seemed to just suck him right in until he was balls deep inside the man. It felt amazing. His cock was surrounded on every side by wet, hot silk that felt like it massaged him when he wasn't even moving.

Ben watched as he slowly pushed his hard cock into Audley's body, then pulled out just as slowly. It was an erotic, intoxicating sight. No matter how he moved, whether slow or fast, the result was the same—fucking intense!

Ben grabbed Audley's ankles and held them in the air, spreading the man's legs as far as they would go. He bent his knees a little and angled his thrusts up more. He knew he hit Audley's sweet spot when the man cried out.

He continued to ram himself into Audley's tight grip, stronger and faster until Audley's entire body shuddered and white spunk shot out of his cock, covering his chest and abdomen. Audley's inner muscles clamped down on Ben, squeezing him forcefully.

Ben groaned, his head falling back on his shoulders. He froze, his body suspended for a brief moment as ecstasy rippled through him. The air rushed from his lungs as he roared out, filling Audley's welcoming body with his release.

Ben fell forward, his arms bracing himself, one on each side of Audley's sweaty body. He dropped his head forward to lean it against Audley's as he felt his knot extend. He knew he was going to be there for a moment. He couldn't think of anywhere else he wanted to be.

"Damn." Audley laughed. "That just gets better and better."

Ben grinned and wiggled his hips until Audley groaned. He knew the knot had attached itself to Audley's prostate. Every movement he made stimulated the walnut-sized gland. Little quick thrusts had Audley whimpering within moments.

Ben gloried in the dazed look glittering in Audley's pale-green eyes. He seemed so shocked by the pleasure coursing through his body, as if he'd never experienced them before. It made Ben feel like the most powerful man on the earth.

Ben's eyes fell down to the pulse beating wildly in Audley's throat. He licked his lips, craving the taste of his mate. "Audley?" he asked huskily. "I want to claim you again."

Audley didn't say anything, just tilted his head to one side in invitation. Ben groaned and sank his canines deep into Audley's throat. The taste that blasted across Ben's tongue as blood filled his mouth was intoxicating.

It was amplified by the loud cry that came from Audley and the wet heat that shot between them. Ben retracted his teeth and licked the bite mark on Audley's shoulder before lifting his head to gaze down at his mate.

Audley looked winded, his face flush, his hair in disarray. Ben didn't think the man had ever looked better. He leaned down and placed a small kiss on Audley's lips. Audley grinned. Ben could feel the man's mouth widening against his lips.

He lifted his head and frowned down at him. "What?"

Audley pointed past Ben's shoulder. Ben turned to see Stefan standing in the kitchen doorway, a smirk on his face and his arms crossed over his chest. Stefan pointed to the cooking oil mess on the floor. "I don't care if the kitchen is my domain. No way in hell am I cleaning that mess up."

Chapter 8

Stefan dipped his head and hid his smile as he watched Audley wipe another trail of flour across his cheek. The man was covered in more flour than he had in the bowl. Audley was a disaster in the kitchen, but he was an enthusiastic disaster.

Stefan hadn't been able to tell his mate no when he begged to learn to cook. Audley wanted to make food for Ben. Stefan agreed, gaining Audley's promise to teach him to carve in exchange.

And then he invited Nate over to help. He could see Nate standing across the kitchen, trying just as hard as Stefan to hide his grin. Stefan believed that everyone had a talent. Audley's talent did not lie in the kitchen.

"Stefan, are you sure this stuff looks right?" Audley asked as he bent over his bowl.

"Did you add the eggs?" Stefan asked.

"Yes, all three of them like you told me to."

Stefan bit his lip as another snicker tried to escape. He had to take just a moment before he could speak again. Audley was looking down at the bowl in front of him like the stuff inside might reach up and bite him.

"Did you add the yeast and sugar?" Stefan finally asked.

"Yes, but it's not rising like you said it would."

"It will," Stefan said. "You have to mix everything together, and then we cover it with a towel and let it rise in a warm place."

"And this makes cinnamon rolls?" Audley sounded skeptical.

"It does."

Audley wiped another trail of flour across his cheek and that seemed to be all it took. Nate started laughing so hard he could barely stand. Stefan had a really hard time holding his laughter in, but he didn't want to hurt Audley's feelings. The man tried so hard.

When Audley grabbed the ball of dough he worked with and held it up in his hands, small globs falling off and hitting the table, Stefan couldn't hold it in anymore. Laughter bubbled out of him and filled the room, joining in with Nate's.

Audley's mouth spread into a thin-lipped smile. Stefan nearly fell over when Audley grabbed a handful of dough and lobbed it at him. It hit Stefan in the face, then fell to the floor with a plop.

Stefan shot Audley a twisted grin and dug his hand into the butter. Audley laughed and tried to dodge the handful of soft goo Stefan tossed at him. He didn't quite make it, butter smattering all over his hair and the side of his face.

Audley grabbed for the container of flour. Stefan went for more butter. He heard Nate laughing hysterically. His hand, full of butter, raised in the air. He cocked an eyebrow at Audley and nodded toward Nate.

Audley grinned. Together they turned and tossed their cooking items at Nate, covering him in butter and flour. Nate sputtered and wiped his eyes. He looked across at Stefan and Audley and then grinned.

That began an all-out war, every man for himself. Butter flew, flour sprinkled, anything and everything that might be a soft projectile was thrown around the room. A few minutes later, the three of them lay on the floor, laughing hysterically.

Stefan glanced around the kitchen and winced. The place looked like a hurricane blew through it. The walls were stained with food, the floors covered. Even the appliances had food all over them.

Not to mention the three men on the floor. Not an inch of their bodies wasn't covered in food. It was in their hair, all over their clothes. There were even food particles under their clothes. They were a mess.

"Oh, lord," Stefan chuckled. "I so do not look forward to cleaning this mess up."

Audley giggled and crawled through the mess to Stefan's side. He reached up and brushed some flour off of Stefan's face before leaning in to kiss him. "I helped make it. I'll help clean it up."

Stefan trailed a hand down the side of Audley's face, wiping away something. He stuck his finger in his mouth, grinning. "Yum, cinnamon filling."

Stefan looked at Audley in amused wonder as the man giggled again, a light, joyous sound that filled the room. It lifted the shadows from Stefan's heart and made him feel carefree and optimistic about the future. It was a sound that Stefan wanted to hear as often as he could.

"You're gorgeous, you know that?"

A flash of stunned disbelief crossed Audley's face as he glanced down at his dirty clothes. "I'm covered in who knows what. I wouldn't exactly call that arousing."

Stefan leaned forward and licked a dollop of sugar and cinnamon mixture off Audley's cheek. "I still think you taste delicious."

"I think you're nuts," Audley said.

Stefan chuckled and started to roll Audley underneath him when he heard the kitchen door open. He glanced up to see a totally shocked look on Ben's face. It sent Stefan into peals of laughter.

"What the hell happened in here?" Ben asked.

"Looks to me like World War Three," Joe said as he stepped in behind Ben. "Are you causing trouble again, baby?"

"Audley started it," Nate protested, amusement clear in his voice. "I was just defending myself."

Ben crossed his arms over his chest and looked across the room. "Audley?"

Stefan's mouth dropped open as a glob of something suddenly hit Ben in the face. Stunned silence filled the room as the large glob of food fell off of Ben's face and hit his uniform. The room was so quiet everyone heard it hit the floor.

Stefan couldn't believe Audley had thrown food at Ben, the biggest, strongest wolf in the pack. He turned to look at him just in time to see the little man scramble to his feet and hightail it out of the room, Ben fast on his heels.

Worried about what might happen, Stefan ignored Joe and Nate as they quickly walked out of the kitchen door and climbed to his feet to run after Ben and Audley. He caught up with them just as Ben tackled Audley to the living room floor. Ben turned them at the last minute so that Audley landed on top of him, and then rolled the smaller man beneath his larger body.

Stefan stopped, his heart pounding frantically as he waited for Ben's reaction. He doubted anyone had ever thrown food at Ben. No one was that brave—or that stupid. He didn't know how Ben would take it.

When Ben leaned down and started licking the food off of Audley's face and laughter filled the room, Stefan's heart started beating normally once again. He stepped into the living room, reaching his mates just as Ben started stripping the man's clothes off.

"You're a mess, love," Ben said. "We need to do something about that."

Stefan grinned and knelt down beside the pair as he reached for the buttons of Ben's shirt. "Need some help?"

* * * *

"So," Nate said as he set a large bag down on the tabletop a couple of weeks later. "I've brought you two a couple of things for tonight."

"Tonight?" Audley asked. "What about tonight?"

"It's the full moon, dummy." Nate frowned. Stefan chuckled at the confusion he could see in Nate's face. "Didn't you explain this to him?"

"I wanted it to be a surprise." Stefan grinned.

"Oh, it will be." Nate snorted.

"Yeah, so what happens tonight?" Audley asked. "What don't I know?"

Nate let out a loud bark of laughter as he started digging into the bag. "Oh, honey, you are in for such a treat. Although, I'm not sure how it works when there's two of you, but I imagine it can't be that much different."

"What happens on the full moon?" Audley demanded.

"Sweetie," Stefan said as he wrapped an arm around Audley's shoulder. Audley was going to be shocked right out of his shoes. "On the full moon, Ben shifts into something a little different, something bigger."

"Bigger?" Audley gulped. "Will he hurt me?"

"Oh, God, no," Nate exclaimed. "It's wonderful. Hell, I have the damn things circled on my calendar. I look forward to the full moon every month. There's nothing quite like it."

"What exactly is *it*?" Audley asked anxiously. "What's going to happen?"

"Ben will shift into something like a werewolf. He will track us down and fuck us so hard we won't walk for a week." Stefan watched Audley's face carefully as he spoke. While he had experienced Ben's full-moon mating, this would be Audley's first time.

Audley seemed to think that over for a moment, and then a smile slowly worked its way across his face. "Cool."

"You have no idea." Nate chuckled. "Which is why I brought you a few *welcome to the pack* presents." Stefan was a bit surprised at the items Nate pulled out of the bag, but he could see where they might be useful. Nate set the items on the table—a large bottle of lube, two butt plugs, and some Epsom salt. Stefan just laughed and shook his head.

Nate held up the two wrapped butt plugs and wiggled his eyebrows. "You might want to go check the fit on these," he said as he handed them over. "I'll just make a pot of tea while I wait."

Stefan almost snickered as Audley turned the butt plug over in his hands, staring at the package as if it were an alien object. He knew Audley lived a very sheltered life with Dane, but surely he'd seen a sex toy before.

"What is it?" Audley asked.

Apparently not! Stefan thought to himself as he walked up the stairs with Audley.

"It's a butt plug, sweetie."

"A butt—why?"

"When Ben shifts tomorrow and tracks us down, he isn't going to have enough control to stretch us out like he normally does. If we use the butt plug, then we're nice and stretched out when he finds us. No pain, just lots of fun."

"How does it work?"

Stefan opened the bedroom door and gestured for Audley to walk in. "I'm just about to show you. Drop your pants and go lie down on the bed."

Audley looked confused, but did as Stefan asked. He dropped his pants on the floor and crawled up on the bed. When he started to roll over onto his back, Stefan reached out and grabbed his leg, stopping him.

"Stay on your hands and knees, Audley," he said. "Not only is it easier this way, but it feels better, too."

Audley nodded and buried his face in his arms, his butt pointing up in the air. Stefan opened the two butt plugs and set them on the bed beside Audley. He grabbed the lube from the bedside drawer and popped the lid open and liberally coated his fingers, then one of the plugs.

Stefan closed the lid and dropped the bottle on the bed. He reached over with his un-lubed hand and caressed the warm, rounded globe of Audley's ass cheek, then gave it a little smack.

"Hold still, sweetie."

Stefan carefully pushed one lubed finger into Audley's tight hole and started moving it in and out. He did this several times, then added a second finger. Audley's body started to tremble as he pushed back against Stefan's intrusive fingers.

"Do you like that, Audley?"

"Yes!" Audley whimpered.

"It's going to get even better." Stefan grabbed the butt plug and pushed it against Audley's tight entrance, gently working it in and out until it slipped inside. Audley cried out, but Stefan knew he wasn't in pain. There was too much pleasure written in the soft glow in his skin and the smile on his face.

Stefan popped the plug in and out several times. He enjoyed the groans coming from his mate. They made him ache all the way down to his toes. He needed more of Audley. "Spread your legs, baby," he said as he patted Audley's thigh.

As soon as Audley spread his legs, Stefan lay down on his back and scooted himself between them until his face was just below Audley's hard cock. He was so close he could stick his tongue out and drag it over the head of Audley's cock...and that's exactly what he did.

"Oh, sweet hell!" Audley groaned. His legs quivered. His cock leaked. His fingers clenched in the sheets. Stefan grinned. He arched his throat and swallowed all of Audley's cock that he could.

He licked, nipped, and sucked at Audley's steel-hard length, all the while shoving the butt plug into the man's ass. He grabbed his own cock with his free hand, unable to stop himself from joining in. He felt so hot and aroused that it took just a few tugs before his entire body seized up.

Stefan groaned loudly around Audley's cock as he erupted, ropes of cum shooting out of his cock to cover his hand and abdomen. He had just a second to inhale a breath before Audley's release filled his mouth with hot seed.

Stefan swallowed as much as he could, chuckling when several drops slid down his chin. A moment later he grunted when Audley collapsed down on top of him. Stefan turned his head and lifted Audley off of him, rolling the man to his back on the mattress.

Scooting up next to him, Stefan gazed down at Audley. He brushed a stray curl back from his face. "Are you okay, baby?"

Audley laughed and shook his head. His pale-green eyes sparkled as he opened them and looked up at Stefan. "I like butt plugs. We need more. We need one for Ben."

Stefan grinned and leaned down to kiss Audley's lips. "I like the way you think, mate."

* * * *

"Audley, Stefan." Audley heard Nate shout from downstairs as they cuddled on the bed. "There's someone here, and they're not knocking to get in."

"Move," Stefan hissed as they both reached for their clothes and got dressed lightening quick. "Who is it?" he asked a little louder.

"I don't know," Nate panted as he reached their room. "It's strange, but they kind of look like older versions of you and Audley."

"Fuck," Stefan replied. "Dane and Oliver found us."

"Nate, do you have your cell phone?" Audley asked, relieved when Nate pulled it out of his pocket. "Call Joe and tell him what's going on. Stefan and I will show you how to get into the attic. They won't know you're here. Both are too stupid to sort out different smells. They just want us."

"I'll call Joe, but there's no way I'm leaving you guys," Nate said as he hit a button on speed dial. They all jumped as they heard the door to the kitchen finally shatter under all the pounding. It seemed that Oliver and Dane finally realized they weren't stupid enough just to let them in. "Joe, it's Nate. I'm at Ben's house with Audley and Stefan. They say Dane and Oliver are here. They just broke into the kitchen. Please hurry. I love you too, Joe."

"All right, if you won't hide in the attic, we'll just have to figure something else out." Audley sighed, cursing that they didn't have time to argue with Nate. At least he and Stefan were vampires. Nate was human. They could handle themselves better than Nate. "Stefan, what about going out the spare bedroom window onto the garage?"

"Nice," Stefan answered, grabbing Nate's hand. Stefan moved quickly and silently. Nate was the one who kept making floorboards creak. They didn't have time to go slowly. Oliver and Dane would follow their scent up here.

Stefan reached and opened the window over the garage as they got to the spare bedroom. "Nate, you first. Hurry."

"Go, go now," Audley whimpered as he heard their brothers hit the bottom of the stairs. "They're coming."

Stefan was out the window a split second after Nate. Audley followed quickly right after him. His heart pounded rapidly as the three of them raced to the end of the garage. He and Stefan jumped down easily.

"Jump, Nate," Stefan hissed as they both spun around to catch him. "Come on, Nate."

"Are you fucking nuts?" Nate answered, his eyes wide with fear. "I'll break my neck."

"We'll catch you. Hurry," Audley said. He watched as Nate turned back toward the window. He must have seen something that made the decision for Nate. He turned back and jumped, landing on Stefan and Audley, who crashed to the ground. They were vampires, but they were small. Nate was the same size as them. *It's hard to catch someone your own weight.*

"There're three of them," Dane yelled from the roof over the garage. Stefan, Audley, and Nate climbed to their feet and started to run. "I think he's human."

"Run for the main road," Nate whispered. Audley was happy he had a plan. Stefan had been here awhile but not as long as Nate. Audley hadn't been here long enough to know the area at all. They each took one of Nate's hands as they ran as fast as they could. "Guys, you're going to pull out my arms."

"I'm sorry, Nate," Stefan panted. "We can't slow down. Our brothers are even faster than we are."

And this was why Nate should have hid in the attic, Audley thought to himself. He was appreciative and loved Nate for wanting to stick together, but in the end, he just slowed them down. Besides, Joe was going to kill them if anything happened to his mate.

"No," Audley screamed as he suddenly felt a heavy body land on him. He hit the ground with a thud, the air rushing from his lungs in a huge gasp. At least he was able to let go of Nate's hand before it happened. "Run!"

"They're not going anywhere." Oliver laughed as he lifted Audley up by his hair. Audley couldn't help but cry out as he felt hair ripping out of his scalp. "Three for the price of two. Guess we'll have to share the third, huh, Dane?"

"Yeah, that works," Dane said, licking the side of Nate's face. He had one hand on Nate's upper arm, the other on Stefan. "I figure my shithead brother and Stefan will be too sore to please us for a while. After they get the beating they deserve for disobeying us and siding with that shifter when we came to get them."

"Fuck you, Dane," Stefan hissed up at the larger vampire. "Stick your dick anywhere near me and I'll bite it off."

"Don't talk to him that way," Oliver growled, smacking Stefan across the face. "He's your mate. I promised you to him."

"We're already mated, you jackass." Audley growled at the sight of his mate being hurt. He turned his head and bit Oliver's arm as hard as he could, keeping his fangs locked in as he tore his head away. Audley wanted to do as much damage as he could so Oliver would let go of him.

"You're going to pay for that," Oliver cried out, dropping him. Audley didn't even have a chance to get to his feet before Oliver grabbed him with his other arm. He saw Nate and Stefan trying to do the same to Dane. Unfortunately, they weren't having any more success. All three of them kicked, bit, and screamed as they were dragged to the SUV that Oliver and Dane came in. "Shut up already!"

"No," Audley yelled, trying to bite Oliver again. This time he got a fist in the face for his troubles. His face ached, but he wasn't going to let Oliver take him without a fight. "I'm not yours!"

"Yes, you are, Audley," Oliver replied as he put Audley in the SUV. "The sooner you get that through your head, the better off you'll be. I'm already going to fuck your ass until you bleed for being with another man. Don't add to the list of offenses you've committed."

"We have to roll," Dane said, lifting his head. Audley cried as he heard sirens in the distance. He knew Joe and Ben wouldn't reach them in time. He grunted as Stefan and Nate were thrown in the backseat on top of him. Seconds later, Oliver and Dane hopped in the front seat and the SUV started moving.

They banged on the windows and tried desperately to open the doors, even as the SUV was moving. Damn child safety locks, Audley thought to himself. There was no use. They were trapped.

Just when the fight seemed to drain out of all three of them, Audley realized where they were going. Oliver and Dane were taking them back to Dane's house. Surely Dane and Oliver realized that would be the first place Ben and Joe would look for them, right?

Knowing Oliver and his brother, their egos thought there was no way Ben could get to them. Audley almost smiled as he thought of what Ben and Joe would do to Oliver and Dane when they found them. He looked over to Stefan and Nate and hoped there was something left of them to find.

Chapter 9

"Audley? Stefan?" Ben yelled out as he headed into the house through the front door. "Nate? Are you guys here?"

"The back door's been obliterated," Joe said, joining him in the living room. "There are large tire tracks by the side of the house, too. They got them, Ben."

"No!" Ben shouted his outrage. "This time they die, and I don't care if it starts a war between werewolves and vampires. They took what is mine."

"I'm calling Devlin," Joe said, but Ben barely heard him. He ran upstairs and checked the rooms, unable to believe his mates were gone. Realizing the worst, he headed back downstairs and bumped into Joe in the kitchen. "Devlin says to drive out to their coven. He's informing Zac of what's going on."

"We use the siren," Ben growled as they headed out the door. A bright glow in the sky caught his attention as he reached for the door handle on the truck. He glanced up, grimacing. "The full moon is soon, Joe."

"I know, Ben. I know," Joe said as they climbed in the truck, "and we'll get them back."

"We better." Ben snarled, then suddenly realized his claws had extended, his canines dropping down. "I'm sorry, Joe. I'm not upset with you, and I'll be forever sorry Nate got pulled into this shit."

"Not your fault, man," Joe answered over the siren as they raced as quickly as they could to the coven. "They will pay for this. I don't give a shit what Zac says. They die for laying a hand on our mates."

"I think Zac will thank us," Ben replied, almost smiling. "I think we'd be doing him a favor."

"It would be my pleasure," Joe said. Ben could see an evil glint in his eyes. He grinned when Joe smiled widely, showing that his teeth were already extending.

This close to the full moon, it wasn't smart to piss off two huge werewolves. Their bodies already wanted to shift into their third form to claim their mates. This type of rage would only set off the change early. Oliver and Dane had no idea what they unleashed.

It took all of Ben's control not to shift as they drove. He could see Joe was having the same problem. Glancing over to the speedometer, he could tell Joe had the cruiser going well over one hundred miles per hour. Ben had focused so much on not changing yet, he barely noticed the time it took to get to the coven.

When they pulled in, it was already dusk. They had maybe a half hour before the change overtook them. Ben met Joe at the front of the patrol vehicle before racing toward the large mansion doors.

"Devlin," Joe said, his voice already changing, as they opened the doors. "What's the word?"

"We asked a lot of the coven members," Devlin answered, his voice more wolf than man as well. "It seems Dane is known for his perversions. He has a torture chamber of sorts at his house. The consensus is that's where they would take your mates."

"Where is it?" Ben growled as he heard his shirt ripping. "How far, Devlin?"

"Oh my, don't attack the vampire," Prince Zacarius said, joining his mate on the front steps. His eyes were wide with amazement as he took in the three werewolves fighting the change. "I'll lead the way. It's not that far. All of our estates are close together."

"We need to hurry, prince," Ben said as he followed after the man. "We're not far from changing and I don't know how much longer we can hold off."

Prince Zacarius eyed Ben from head to foot, then nodded his head. "Yes, I can see that. Very well, gentlemen, try to keep up."

Ben blinked as Prince Zacarius took off like a shot. One second he stood in front of Ben, the next he was halfway to the woods. Damn, the man was fast. Ben grinned, clenched his fists, and turned his head from side to side as he popped his neck.

He could feel the moon's pull like bugs crawling under his skin. He held on to his control by a thread, barely keeping himself from shifting. Rage barreled through his body. It was equaled by the need to find his mates and claim them.

Ben turned and grinned at Joe and Devlin as the need to hunt filled him. Oliver and Dane just became the prey to three werewolves. They were dead men, and they didn't even know it. They would.

Letting out a loud howl, Ben took off after Prince Zacarius. The scent of the night air combining with the fragrance of the woods and the grass beneath his feet filled his senses. It was intoxicating, exhilarating. The faster Ben ran, the more scents he encountered.

He could feel his claws extend more. Fur began to sprout from under his skin, and his head ached as pointed ears grew out the top. He was shifting and he couldn't stop it, not this time. The moon's pull was too strong to resist.

Coming to a clearing in the woods, Ben paused. He could see lights off in the distance, just beyond the clearing, and knew that was his destination. That which he sought was inside the same brick building as the lights.

Ben lifted his nose into the air and sniffed. Again, the fragrance of the woods wafted through him. He sniffed again and again, searching for something. Just as he was about to give up, Ben caught a faint scent so glorious, his knees shook.

Ben growled low and inhaled deep. The sweet, alluring fragrance of his mates surrounded Ben, filled him, made him ache to touch his mates and claim them. Rage that they weren't standing right in front of him burned through Ben.

He glanced at the two werewolves beside him. Joe watched the lit house with dogged determination. Joe had shifted into his third form just like Ben and flexed his clawed hands as he gazed at the house.

Devlin, while he shifted, too, seemed to have eyes only for Prince Zacarius. For his part, the prince looked right back at Devlin, a sensual grin on his lips. Ben could smell the mating heat between the two men. It made him ache to hold his own mates.

"Let's go," Ben said in a deep gravelly voice. He started walking slowly toward the house, his anger building with every step. His mates should be within reach of him when the full moon mating came about. How dare Oliver and Dane interfere with that.

Joe stepped into line beside Ben as they both crept toward the house. He could hear Prince Zacarius and Devlin arguing behind him, but couldn't have cared less what they argued about. Getting to his mates and killing the men who took them was his first priority.

Ben stopped at the edge of the house and cocked his head to one side, listening. He could hear crickets chirping in the distance, the sound of a leaky pipe dripping, but nothing else. It was like the place was deserted. Not a sound could be heard from inside the building.

"Walk carefully, Ben," the prince said. "Oliver and Dane will be able to smell you coming. A vampire has a very strong sense of smell."

"So do I," Ben growled. He crept along the side of the house until he came to a door. He turned the handle, not surprised to find the door locked. Gripping it tighter, Ben turned the doorknob until he heard the lock snap and the door opened.

He cocked his head to one side again to listen and then walked inside when he heard nothing. He found himself standing in a well-maintained kitchen. His only interest in the place was the door Prince Zacarius pointed to.

"Is that the basement door?" the prince asked.

Ben crossed the room to the thick wooden door. Again, he found the door locked. Another quick turn of the handle broke the lock, and the door swung open. Ben could barely stop his gasp of shock as he stepped back from the doorway.

So many scents wafted up the stairwell leading down that it was hard to separate them all. Ben could smell fear, heartache, and pain. It was overshadowed by the stench of blood and sweat.

Ben crinkled his nose in distaste. He could feel his claws digging into the wood surrounding the doorframe. If the blood he smelled came from one of his mates, Ben would rip Oliver and Dane limb from limb.

Ben sniffed the air once more and then slowly stepped down the steep stairwell. He sniffed the air with each step. Ben wasn't about to let Oliver or Dane creep up on him. The plan was for things to happen the other way around.

The bottom of the stairwell opened up into a small landing area. Three gray stone-walled hallways led off from this point. Ben walked to the entrance of each hallway and sniffed the air until the scent of his mates was the strongest.

He pointed down the hallway he intended to go down, getting a nod from Joe, Devlin, and the prince. He stepped carefully down the hallway, not putting Dane above booby trapping the floor or walls. He wouldn't put anything past the bloodsucker.

The first door Ben came to was unlocked, which surprised him. He listened for a moment, then pushed the wooden door open. It looked like a storage room, with shelves lining the walls and boxes stacked in every bit of floor space. Ben sniffed the air, and then shut the door when he detected no scent of his mates inside.

The next door was several feet farther down the hallway. And it was locked from the outside this time. Ben inhaled. The scent of Stefan was very strong. He pressed his ear to the thick wood and listened.

Ben's heart pounded painfully in his chest when he heard whimpering through the wood. He instantly knew Stefan made the small cries. There was no mistaking the tone of Stefan's voice, even when he cried.

Ben clenched his teeth to keep from growling as he unlocked the door. His mate was inside that room. Nothing—and no one—would keep him out. It was all he could do to stop himself from letting his rage loose and kicking the door in as he really wanted to do.

The sight that met Ben's eyes as he opened the door and peered inside took all of the air from his lungs. He stood frozen to the spot in shock as he watched his very naked mate swing from a large hook in the ceiling. His hands were tied together, looped over the hook.

"Stefan?"

Stefan started wiggling, his cries getting louder as he struggled against the bonds around his wrists. Ben hurried over and wrapped his hands around Stefan's waist. He turned Stefan until their eyes met.

"Ben!" Stefan cried out. "Oh, my God, Ben. Oli–Oliver and D–Da–Dane, they have Audley."

"I know, baby," Ben replied. "Joe, Devlin, and the prince are here with me. We're going to get you out of here."

Ben quickly looked at the contraption holding his mate, trying to figure out the quickest and least painful way of freeing Stefan. He finally grabbed the latch attached to the wrist restraints on Stefan's arms and pulled until they snapped.

Stefan fell down into his arms with a small grunt. Ben hugged the man for just a moment, inhaling his strong scent, and then set him on his feet. "Find your clothes, baby, and get dressed. We need to go find Audley and Nate."

Stefan sniffled and shook his head. "Dane cut my clothes off of me. I don't have anything to wear."

Stefan's words only increased Ben's anger. No one should see either of his mates naked, ever. He whipped his shirt over his head and handed it to Stefan. It had a few rips and tears but it would cover most of the man.

Once Stefan was sufficiently covered, Ben grabbed his hand and pulled him toward the door. He peeked out to make sure no one was coming, then continued down the hallway to find his other mate.

Audley's scent was strongest at the door at the end of the hallway. Ben paused outside the door and listened once again. He frowned when he heard a strange noise that he couldn't immediately define. But he did recognize the sounds of Audley crying out.

Ben pushed Stefan to the side of the door, flattening him against the wall. He took a deep breath to calm himself, then pushed the door open and stepped inside the room. The sight that met his eyes was even more horrific than finding Stefan dangling from a hook in the ceiling.

Audley hung from the ceiling just as Stefan had, naked and crying. Only this time, Oliver stood there, a long black leather whip in his hands. Ben's eyes went from the whip to the deep red marks marring Audley's pale skin.

He growled and unleashed the beast fighting to get out and protect his mates. Leaping across the room, Ben dove at Oliver. The man was surprised by his entrance just long enough for Ben to reach him, but the moment Ben's teeth latched on to his arm, Oliver started fighting back.

Ben felt several kicks to his legs and stomach. He ignored the pain they brought and ripped into Oliver. He didn't care what Prince Zacarius said. He didn't care that this attack might start up the war between werewolves and vampires. He just cared about killing Oliver, the man who took his mates.

Ben was determined that Oliver would never have the chance to attack his mates again—no matter what happened to him. He could hear shouting, but it was muted, as if coming from a great distance. It didn't seem important, so Ben ignored it and renewed his attack on Oliver, striking out with his claws.

Pain exploded in Ben's body. It stunned him enough for Oliver to pull away. Ben looked down at his shoulder, surprised to see a trail of blood dripping down his arm from a small wound..

He turned to glare at Oliver. "You took that which did not belong to you. Now you will die." Ben said it so matter-of-factly that he could see Oliver's eyes widen in fear. As far as he was concerned, Oliver was already dead. His body just hadn't caught up yet.

"Audley is mine!" Oliver snapped. "By our laws, his brother gave him to me."

"Audley is my mate!"

"You're a dog!" Oliver shouted. "We do not *mate* with dogs."

"I am a werewolf, a soldier for the Wolf Creek Pack," Ben snapped. "I know all about what is and is not lawful with werewolves and vampires. By your laws and mine, once Audley mated me, he belonged to me and you know it."

"He's mine!" Oliver shouted. "I claim him by right of family endowment."

"He's been mated!" Ben shouted right back. "Your claim is no longer valid!"

Ben took a step toward Oliver, pausing when Oliver moved his hand and revealed the gun he held. He could smell the silver in the gun and knew Oliver had prepared to kill him from the very beginning.

He didn't mind dying to save his mates. He'd do anything for them—even if it meant his life. Stefan and Audley would still have each other, and they would be safe because Ben had every intention of taking Oliver down with him.

Ben took another step toward Oliver, then another. Oliver raised the gun and fired just as he lunged. A sharp pain entered his chest, blossoming outward until Ben almost passed out from the intensity.

But he couldn't overlook the hatred in Oliver's eyes, the gleam of insanity. He knew if he didn't kill Oliver, his mates would suffer from it. Ben pushed the pain to the back of his mind and went for Oliver again.

He swung out with one hand, exhilaration spiraling through him when his claws connected, ripping a large gash in Oliver's chest. He swung out with the other hand, just missing Oliver as the man jumped back.

Ben growled and raised his clawed hand once more. He started to bring it down, aiming for Oliver's neck, when the man turned the gun in his hand toward Audley's dangling body. Ben froze. His heart pounded frantically.

"Move and he's dead," Oliver snapped.

"He'd rather be dead than left with you," Ben replied, hoping it was true. Well, he was pretty sure it was true. Audley seemed to hate Oliver and Dane.

"So be it."

Ben watched Oliver's fingers pull on the trigger as if in slow motion. He knew he'd only get one shot at this. Either he would die in the process or Audley would. Ben leapt into the air and dove at Oliver, putting his body between the bullet and Audley's dangling form.

He heard a loud scream and the bang of a gun just before he felt a searing pain in his chest. The momentum of his leap carried him to Oliver even as the bullet entered his chest. He swiped at Oliver's neck and had the satisfaction of seeing gushes of Oliver's blood spurt out.

Oliver dropped the gun and grabbed at his throat, his eyes looking wild, desperate. Even as he sank back onto the floor, Ben watched, knowing that he had done what he set out to do. Oliver was dead.

The pain in Ben's chest weighed him down. He felt dizzy and out of breath. All of the strength in his body seemed to be slowly seeping away with the blood that dripped from his numerous wounds.

Ben had just enough strength to turn his head and look at his mates. He could see Devlin and Stefan helping Audley down to the floor. Stefan quickly ripped the restraints off of Audley's wrists, and then both men scrambled over to kneel next to him.

"Don't you dare die on me, Benjamin Nobles," Stefan whispered. "You promised to always take care of me and you can't do that if you die."

Ben smiled weakly. "Love you so much, both of you."

"Then stay with us," Audley said.

Ben frowned at the tears he could see sliding down Audley's delicate face. He reached over and wiped one away. "No crying, little one," he said. "You're safe now."

"I'll never be safe without you, Ben," Audley said.

"You have Stefan," Ben reasoned. "He'll take care of you."

"No!" Audley shouted as he wiped at his tears. He surprised Ben. Audley didn't shout very often, if ever. "You're supposed to be the center that we gravitate around, remember? How can we do that if you leave us?"

Ben could feel himself weakening from the loss of blood. He knew he only had a few moments more with his beloved mates. He took in as much of their beautiful features as he could, hoping that he would remember them in the afterlife.

"Love you both," he murmured, then slowly closed his eyes. Ben could hear Stefan and Audley cry out his name, both of them shouting, but the sound grew farther and farther away until Ben heard nothing at all.

Chapter 10

"No! Ben!" Audley shouted as Ben's eyes closed. He lightly smacked the side of Ben's face but received no response, not even the flicker of an eyelid. "Ben, wake up! Ben!"

His brows drew together in an agonized expression. He wasn't going to lose Ben—not after finding him. He loved Stefan more than his next breath, but Audley needed both of his mates. Ben was just as much a part of him as Stefan.

Audley smacked Ben a little harder. "Damn it, Ben! Wake the fuck up. We're bonded now. We die when you do, remember? We need you."

"Audley!"

Audley glanced up at Stefan's shocked face. If he hadn't been so scared, he might have felt embarrassed, but right now he was too worried about Ben. "Help me," he pleaded.

"Audley," Stefan said sadly. "He's been shot with silver bullets. Can't you smell it? He can't heal from that kind of injury."

"He can if we dig the bullets out," Audley insisted. "We can give him our blood to replace the blood he's lost, as much as he needs."

Stefan looked back down at Ben. "Dig the bullets out?"

Audley frowned. Stefan asked his question in such a way that it seemed like he had never thought about digging the bullets out. "Yes, we dig the bullets out. Once the silver is out of his body, we can use our blood to help him heal."

Audley grabbed Stefan by the arm and shook him. "We have to do something, Stefan. I'm not ready to give him up."

Stefan nodded and looked at Ben's wounds. He still looked confused. Audley snorted and pushed him back. He flicked one finger up and extended his claw as far as it would go. Praying Ben slept through it, Audley stuck his finger in the hole in Ben's chest and rooted around until he felt the bullet.

He knew the moment he touched the silver bullet. His finger burned, the stench of smoldering flesh filling the room. Audley ignored the pain as he knew Ben had done and dug until he got a claw under the edge of the bullet. He pulled back slowly until the small silver glob popped free and fell to the floor.

"Get your blood in that wound, Stefan," Audley ordered as he reached into the next bullet hole. As he dug for it, he could see Stefan bite a large gash into his wrist, then dribble blood over Ben's wound.

Audley dropped the second bullet to the floor and leaned over to dig for the third. He glanced over at Ben's chest wound, his heart racing faster when he saw the wound starting to heal.

Audley worked harder, digging until he found the last silver bullet and pulled it out. He tossed this one across the room and forgot it the moment it left his hand. His entire world rested on the soft rise and fall of Ben's chest.

"Is it working?"

Audley glanced up to see Prince Zacarius standing over them. Next to him stood a werewolf. Audley assumed it was Devlin by the close way he hovered over the prince. He shook his head. "I don't know. We got the bullets out, but I just don't know."

"We need to get him upstairs. I've called for a car to take him back to my estate," Prince Zacarius said. "I have a special doctor standing by, one who has dealt with our kind before. He should be able to tell us if it worked."

Audley bent his head over, wiped his tears away, and nodded. "Okay, let's move him, but we have to be very careful so we don't cause any more damage."

"I think Joe and I should be able to lift him without too much difficulty," Devlin said in a gravelly voice.

Audley frowned, his eyebrows drawing together as he glanced around the room for the other werewolf. "Where is Joe?"

Devlin pointed over his shoulder. "He went after Nate."

"And Dane?" Audley asked. "Did Joe stop Dane?"

"Dane?"

Audley closed his eyes briefly. When he opened them again, everyone was staring at him in confusion. Audley grimaced. "Dane and Oliver put Stefan in the other room, and then brought me in here. Oliver stayed here with me, but Dane took Nate off somewhere else."

"Shit!" Devlin exclaimed as he headed out the door.

Audley jumped to his feet. He gestured to Ben. "Get him upstairs. Devlin doesn't know this place like I do. He's liable to get lost in all of these rooms. I have a pretty good idea of where Dane took Nate."

He started for the door when Stefan reached out and grabbed his wrist. "Audley, how do you know where Dane took Nate?"

"This isn't my first time down here," Audley replied. He heard Stefan's quick inhale and watched the way his face paled. Audley reached up and caressed the side of Stefan's face. "It's okay, Stefan. You and Ben took me away from this."

"But Audley," Stefan said. Audley knew what Stefan saw as he glanced around the room, the ropes and chains, the hook in the ceiling, the whips that hung in a line on the wall. It was a chamber of horrors. "You've been here before?" Stefan asked. "In this room specifically?"

Audley nodded. "Oliver would bring me down here when he came over for dinner. He said he was training me to belong to him, to obey to his every command." Audley shrugged. "I guess it didn't take because I still got away from him."

Stefan's hand shook as he pushed it through his hair. "Fuck, Audley. You should have told me what was going on. I could have—I could have—"

"There was nothing you could have done, Stefan," Audley said. "Neither of us is strong enough to take on Oliver or Dane. That's why we need Ben so much. He loves us enough to keep us safe."

Audley almost laughed over the frown that covered Stefan's face, but he didn't think now was the time for laughter.

"That's why you weren't afraid when they brought us down here," Stefan whispered. "You knew Ben would come for us, didn't you?"

Audley crossed his arms over his chest as he nodded his head. "Ben said he would always take care of us, keep us safe. I knew he would come for us. He's our mate. He wouldn't leave us down here to be abused by Oliver and Dane."

"You have so much faith in a man you've only known for a few weeks?" Prince Zacarius said from behind Audley.

Audley turned to face the prince. "Of course," he said. "Didn't you trust Devlin once you knew he was your mate?"

"Just checking." Prince Zacarius chuckled as he held up his hand. "Besides, Stefan already gave me a dressing down the last time I said anything about Ben. I just wanted to make sure you felt the same."

"Without Ben and Stefan, I am nothing, I have nothing," Audley said simply. "They are my reason for living."

"Audley," Stefan whispered, tears in his eyes.

Audley could see the stunned amazement on his face. He smiled and backed up toward the door. "Get Ben upstairs. I'll go find our friends."

"I'd appreciate it if you could bring my mate back to me in one piece," the prince hollered as Audley darted out the door. "I'm kind of attached to him."

Audley had to hope that Prince Zacarius and Stefan could get Ben up the stairs to safety. With Dane running around loose, everyone that stayed downstairs would be in danger. Audley knew Oliver wasn't nearly as sadistic as his brother. Oliver just played at being sadistic. Dane was evil right down to his bones.

Audley made his way back down the hallway he'd come through earlier, to the next hallway. There were three hallways that led off of the main entrance, but the one in the middle led to the rooms Dane liked to use the most, the rooms where the worst was done.

Audley held no doubt that his brother had taken Nate to one of those rooms. He just needed to figure out exactly which one. That question was answered for Audley when a door halfway down the hallway abruptly shattered and two men came flying through, fighting.

Dane was easily identifiable. He was the only one in human form. The other man, er, werewolf—wasn't so easy. Audley didn't know if it was Joe or Devlin, as they both looked similar in shifted appearance.

It didn't matter to Audley who it was, Joe or Devlin. Both were friends and Audley knew he needed to help. He just wasn't sure what he could do. Audley couldn't shift, and he certainly wasn't as large as Dane.

Audley suddenly remembered the whips that Dane kept in one of the other rooms. One in particular came to mind. Audley shuddered as he remembered the long leather straps with bits of sharp metal attached to the ends.

He also remembered the pain those little metal shards produced. While it gave him the willies to even touch the damn thing, a part of him would be overjoyed to use it on the man who had used it on him.

Audley raced back down the hallway and into the first room. The black leather whip hung from the wall, right where Audley remembered it. He reached up and grabbed it off the wall, then turned and ran back out into the hallway.

The fight had apparently gone back into the room, because the hallway was deserted, but Audley could still hear growling and grunts. He followed the noises to the shattered door and looked inside. Sure enough, Dane and the werewolf were still fighting and they were both a mass of cuts, scratches, and blood.

Audley took just a moment to look around the room as he stepped inside. As he did, he realized that the werewolf fighting Dane was Devlin because Joe lay crumpled in a heap in the corner. He'd shifted back to human form.

Audley rushed to his side and checked his pulse. He heaved a sigh of relief when he found one, strong and steady. A quick check for injuries and Audley found a small bump on the back of Joe's head. There was no blood. Whatever made the bump hadn't even broken the skin, just knocked the larger man out cold.

Hearing a whimper, Audley looked up and found Nate staring down at him, tears on his cheeks. He quickly crossed over to the man and tried to get him down off the hook in the ceiling, cursing to himself when he found he was too short to reach.

"I'm sorry, Nate," Audley said. "I can't get you down yet. I'll look for something, though." Audley started to turn away when Nate whimpered again. He looked back, smiling when he saw the worried frown on Nate's face. "Joe's fine, Nate. He just has a little bump on the head."

"Can you wake him up?" Nate whispered. "He can get me down."

Audley wasn't so sure of that. Joe might be strong, but he had also been knocked over the head. Audley doubted the man could do anything—even if he was conscious. Still, he could at least wake the man up.

Audley looked around the room and spotted a bottle of water in the far corner. Unfortunately, it was on the other side of the fight. He walked to the wall and moved slowly around the edge of the room, avoiding the fight as much as possible. It wasn't easy.

Dane and Devlin were in a knock-down, drag-out fight for their lives. Between the sharp-clawed swipes with their hands and the sharp fangs, blood flew everywhere. By the time Audley reached the bottle of water, he looked like he'd been directly involved in the fight.

Getting back to Nate was even harder. One stray swipe of Devlin's claws caught him in the upper arm. Audley cried out. He jumped back, leaving a smear of blood on the wall as he fell against it.

He covered the deep gash with his free hand, wincing as pain radiated down his arm. He could feel warm blood seep through his fingers. It wasn't a death blow by any means, but it sure hurt like hell.

Audley tried to ignore the pain, push it to the back of his mind. He needed to get back to Nate and Joe. Standing to his feet, he started around the edge of the room again. It took him a few minutes, but he finally knelt down next to Joe.

Audley uncapped the water bottle and poured the contents out onto Joe's face. Joe just started to stir when Audley heard a low, deep, ominous laugh behind him. He turned slowly, his eyes widening when he saw Dane standing behind him, Devlin in an unmoving slump on the floor at Dane's feet.

Audley's first thought was that Prince Zacarius was going to be pissed at him. He had failed to protect the prince's mate and bring him back. His second thought as he watched Dane advance on him was that there wasn't going to be anything left of him for the prince to tear apart. Dane was going to do that for him.

"Well, well, little brother." Dane growled. "It seems you've been very bad." Dane cracked his knuckles together, one hand fisted into the palm of the other. Audley almost snorted at the bad mafia-movie stance.

"You're such a drama queen, Dane."Audley knew he was going to die from the way Dane's eyes narrowed to small slits as he stepped closer. He just didn't care. Audley had spent most of his life being afraid of his older brother. He was done.

"You know you're going to pay for that statement, don't you?"

Audley rolled his eyes. "Yeah, yeah, you're the big, bad boogeyman and I should be shaking in my boots." Audley stuck out a bare leg and wiggled his toes at Dane. "Sorry, not wearing any boots. Maybe you could catch me tomorrow. I'll make sure to buy a pair."

Audley had the satisfaction of seeing Dane's eyes widen just before he was backhanded across the face. *So, the pain begins*, Audley thought to himself. He'd experienced Dane's punishments in the past and before him, from his fathers. He was well versed in the art of discipline.

Only this time, he wasn't going to blindly take it like he had in the past. Stefan and Ben had both shown him that he deserved better. He was worthy of someone's respect, love, and caring. He didn't have to be Dane's punching boy anymore.

Audley climbed to his feet and stood up straight before Dane, looking him right in the eye. The momentary pause in Dane's stance gave him strength. He'd never stood up to his brother before. Audley knew Dane had to be stunned.

"I've had enough of you hitting me, Dane," he said, pleased with how even his voice sounded. "I'm mated now, and you no longer have the right to discipline me in any way, shape, or form."

Dane stared for a moment, then seemed to regain his composure. "You dare speak to me this way? Have you forgotten everything you've ever been taught?"

"I haven't forgotten a damn thing, Dane," Audley snapped. "Not the times you hung me from the ceiling for hours on end, not the whippings or beatings, nothing. I remember every little thing you ever did to me." Audley took a step toward his brother. "And I'm not going to take it anymore."

Audley winced and dropped to one knee when Dane backhanded him again. He cradled his aching cheek for a moment and took a deep breath, wishing one of his mates were here. As he reached up to push his hair from his eyes, he suddenly remembered the whip he held in his other hand.

He stood to his feet again and glared at Dane. He gripped the handle of the whip, holding it close to his side. "I told you that you don't have the right to punish me anymore, Dane. Are you so stupid that you don't understand my words?"

Audley swung the whip at his brother, using all of the strength in his arm. The leather strips wrapped around Dane's body. Audley knew the moment the metal shards connected with Dane's back as well. The man arched forward, crying out in pain.

Audley yanked back on the whip, knowing from experience that the metal would dig deep and leave painful gashes in Dane's flesh. He swung again and again, losing track of anything but the agonized cries from his brother.

He snarled and bared his fangs when the whip was suddenly ripped out of his hand. Intending to bite into whoever took the item, he turned, stopping suddenly when he found Ben standing before him. Considering the larger and hairier version of Ben he'd seen in the other room, Audley was a little surprised to see Ben back in human form.

"He's dead, baby," Ben said gently. "You can stop now."

Tilting his head back, he stared at Ben in confusion. "Dead?"

"Yes, baby. Dane and Oliver are both gone. They can't hurt you again."

"But—" Audley turned around and stared down at the bloody body at his feet. Dane really was dead. There was no way anyone— even a vampire—could live with the amount of blood covering Dane's body.

Audley stared at the deep gashes, broken bones, and blood dripping onto the floor in horror. He did this. He took someone else's life—his brother's at that. Nausea welled up inside of Audley. He covered his mouth and ran to the corner of the room. Falling to his knees, Audley lost the contents of his stomach, which, admittedly, wasn't much.

As he wiped his hand across his mouth, Audley felt a hand smooth the hair back from his forehead. He turned to see Stefan squatting down beside him. Another larger body pressed up against his back.

"How are you feeling?" Stefan asked.

"I killed Dane."

"I think he kind of deserved it, Audley," Stefan said softly. "He certainly wasn't going to let you out of here, and who knows what he had planned for Nate. You probably saved Nate's life."

Audley shook his head. "Joe was waking up. He would have saved Nate."

"Joe can't even stand up," said a voice from across the room. Audley glanced over to see Nate kneeling on the floor next to Joe, who had his head cradled in his hands. "If he moves too much, his head might explode."

Joe apparently had enough strength to lift his head and glare at Nate. Audley couldn't help but smile when the glare sent Nate into peals of laughter. Still, he was glad to see the grin on Joe's face right before he made a grab for Nate, kissing him.

"What about Devlin?" Audley asked as he continued looking around the room. "Is he okay?"

"My mate is fine, Audley," Prince Zacarius said from several feet away where he held Devlin's head in his lap. Devlin, too, was back in human form. "I do thank you for ensuring that he returned to me, although I would have appreciated a little less wear and tear on his body."

"Sorry," Audley replied.

"I do not hold you at fault, Audley," the prince said. "Devlin did this all on his own. He was aching for a good fight and he found one. Didn't you, my love?"

Audley snickered when Devlin rolled his eyes. He looked back to Stefan and Ben. "What about you two?" he asked. "Are you okay? I thought you were going to go back to the prince's estate where a doctor could look at you. I thought you were dying, Ben."

"Do you really think I would leave you here alone, Audley?" Ben asked. "I'm not safe until you and Stefan are safe, remember? We're bonded. I can't live without the two of you." He grinned, which surprised Audley considering the condition he'd last seen his mate in. "Besides, it's the full moon mating tonight. Werewolves have been known to chew through steel to get to their mates on the full moon. Do you really think a few bullet holes are going to keep me from you and Stefan?"

Audley frowned as he looked over Ben's body. The wounds on his chest and shoulders seemed to be healing, but they were still pink and puckered. They looked painful. "Are you really in any condition to be thinking about sex right now? Shouldn't you be in bed or something?"

Ben's golden eyes held a sensuous glint in them as he grinned again. "I like the way you think, mate, but at this point, I'd settle for a flat surface."

"Ben!" Audley exclaimed.

"Audley, it's the full moon," Ben said. "Not mating you and Stefan tonight will hurt far worse than a silver bullet."

"You need bed rest."

"The only thing I need is you and Stefan."

Audley frowned. He was trying to understand this full moon mating thing, but the injuries to his mate seemed to overshadow everything. Audley could only think of getting Ben into bed where he could heal, not have sex. However...

"Fine, but I refuse to be claimed in this house," Audley said. "Take me back to the prince's estate." Anything to get Ben in bed where he could rest.

Audley was a little astonished at the strength Ben displayed as he was pulled to his feet. Maybe Ben was healing faster than Audley thought. That didn't mean Audley wasn't still worried, though. He wouldn't be satisfied until the pink flesh on Ben's chest healed all the way.

"Let's find something to cover you up with first," Ben said. "I'd prefer that only Stefan and I see you as you are."

"Ben, everyone in the room has seen me naked by now."

"I know," Ben growled.

Audley rolled his eyes and went in search of his clothing. They were in tatters, but they'd cover him until he could find something else to wear.

The trip up the stairs took more time than Audley would have liked. He wanted out of Dane's house as fast as he could go. He may have grown up here but he hated every brick of the place. It didn't hold anything but bad memories for him. If he had his way, the place would be torn down, never to be built again. Maybe turned into a park or something.

The small group limping out of the house was met by a group of vampire soldiers. Audley vaguely remembered Prince Zacarius saying he had sent for his people. The only thing that Audley got out of that information was the two large black SUVs sitting in front of the house, doors open.

Audley quickly helped Stefan and Ben inside. The moment the doors closed, the driver started the vehicle and drove them back to the coven estate. Audley didn't start breathing normally until they pulled in the gates. His relief felt like a physical weight lifted off of his chest. They were finally safe.

Albert met them at the door. More people gathered around to help them all upstairs to the blue room once again. The quick way Ben walked into the room and shut the door behind the three of them, stripping his clothes off, made Audley's worry for the man skyrocket until he saw him start to shift again.

Right before Audley's eyes, Ben grew bigger. His face elongated slightly, pointed ears grew out of the top of his head, and fur covered his entire body. What shocked Audley the most was the large cock that jutted out from Ben's groin. He thought Ben was large before. He was wrong. Now, Ben was huge.

Audley started shaking his head when Ben turned in his direction and sniffed the air, a low growl coming from the man's furry chest.

"Mine!"

"Shit!" Audley croaked out.

"I told you that butt plug would come in handy." Stefan snickered next to him as he started undressing. Stefan paused, arching an eyebrow at Audley. "You might want to get naked and find the lube. We're going to need it."

"He needs a doctor," Audley said as he pointed to Ben.

"He needs us," Stefan replied.

"Stef—" Audley's words dwindled away when Ben stalked over and started sniffing his neck. Large clawed hands grabbed his hips. A long, rough tongue scraped up the side of Audley's neck, making him shiver in response.

"Mine," Ben growled again.

Audley couldn't help leaning into the strong body behind him. Even covered in fur, Ben felt wonderful against his backside. When Ben's tongue started licking over his skin again, Audley titled his head to one side. He knew he should insist that Ben see a doctor but it just felt so good when Ben touched him.

"Ben, what—" Audley started to asked when one sharp claw began to shred what was left of his clothing. In a matter of moments, Audley was naked, his ripped and torn clothing in a pile at his feet. Another moment later and Stefan's naked body pressed against his front, sandwiching Audley between his mates.

Audley wanted to protest, really he did, but being pressed between the naked bodies of his mates, knowing that they had all survived their run in with Dane and Oliver, made any words he might have spoken dwindle away to be replaced by a deep moan.

"Come on, baby," Stefan said as he grabbed Audley's hand and started pulling him toward the bed. "We need to get ourselves stretched out before Ben can claim us."

Audley stumbled to the bed, glancing over his shoulder at Ben. "But what about Ben?"

"He gets to watch." Stefan chuckled. "I don't imagine he'll be able to last too long. Maybe we should make it a contest, huh? See how long Ben can last before he loses control and attacks us?"

"He's going to attack us?" Audley squeaked as Stefan pushed him down on the bed.

"Only in a good way, love."

Audley turned to look at Ben again. His eyes nearly bugged out of his head when he found Ben standing at the end of the bed, his golden eyes watching him and Stefan intently. He had his cock in his hand and was stroking it slowly, baring his teeth and growling softly.

"Mine!"

"Does he ever say anything other than that?"

"Not really," Stefan said. "At least not until he's shifted back."

"And when does that happen?"

"Only after he's claimed us."

Audley inhaled sharply, his eyes darting back to Stefan when he felt two lubed fingers press into his ass. He expected one to start off with, not two. Stefan chuckled.

"Sorry, love, we don't have time to go slow. Our wolf isn't going to wait long before he's on us. The quicker we do this, the quicker he gets us."

Audley rolled his eyes and held out his hand. "Fine, give me the lube and swing your ass around here. I can get you ready while you get me ready."

"I do like the way you think, baby." Stefan grinned and slapped the bottle of lube into Audley's hand.

Audley flipped open the lid and squirted some lube out on his fingers. By the time he had the bottle closed Stefan had swung around, straddling Audley's head. Audley was a little unsure of what to do. Not that he didn't know how to stretch Stefan after all this time, but the man's hard cock hung right in front of his face. Audley felt a deep need to suck the man's cock.

Deciding to go with his urges, Audley opened his mouth and swallowed Stefan's cock at the same time he pushed two fingers into the man's ass. Stefan shuddered, a long, lust-filled moan coming from him. Audley sucked harder, the sound of his mate arousing him quickly to a fever pitch. It didn't hurt that Stefan added another finger to his ass, shoving all three inside.

The sound of Ben's growls grew louder. Audley could see him just out of the corner of his eye. The strokes to Ben's cock were getting quicker, the man's furry chest moving faster. Audley was pretty sure he and Stefan had just a few moments more before Ben joined them.

He just barely got another two fingers into Stefan's ass when Ben lost his control and attacked. One moment, Audley was stretching Stefan, the man's cock deep inside his mouth. The next moment, he was rolled to his hands and knees being fucked with such force that it pushed him up the bed. Audley barely had time to blink let alone breath.

"Mine!" Ben growled. That was Audley's only warning before long canine teeth sank into his neck. Audley cried out, the sensation of being fucked into the mattress and claimed at the same time igniting a fire in his body that almost instantly exploded into a haze of burning lust.

His cock erupted, white cream shooting all over the bedspread. Audley's arms gave out, and he crashed down onto the bed as Ben extracted his teeth. He turned his head to see Ben pull away from him and go after Stefan. Ben grabbed their mate, flipped him over, and sank into Stefan's ass, pounding away almost immediately.

Audley would have thought he might feel left out or pushed aside after Ben left him so quickly. He was surprised to find himself getting turned on again by the sight of Ben claiming Stefan. It was a beautiful sight. Stefan had his legs wrapped around Ben's waist, his arms around Ben's neck. Stefan's head was arched back as Ben's teeth sank into him. He cried out, but it seemed to be a sound of joy, not pain.

Audley suddenly wanted in on the claiming in a way he never did before. He grabbed the bottle of lube and squirted some more out on his fingers, tossing the bottle to the bed before crawling over to kneel behind Ben.

Audley didn't know if this was allowed. It never really came up during the time they had been together. Stefan and Audley took turns claiming each other, but Ben was usually the one doing the claiming of either of them. They had never claimed Ben. Audley figured it was time…at least he hoped so.

Audley watched for any reaction out of Ben as he pushed a finger into the man's ass. He wasn't sure what he expected, maybe Ben to argue and say no. It certainly wasn't the reaction he received. Ben roared and started pumping his hips faster. His thrusts seemed to become longer, harder, as if he was trying to impale himself on Audley's finger. Audley added another one.

"Yes!" Ben shouted. Audley grinned and started thrusting his fingers into Ben's tight grip faster and faster. When he added a third finger, Ben's body began to tremble. Audley heard Stefan cry out. Then Ben grunted. His movements suddenly slowed, but just for a moment, and then he sped up again. "Audley, now, love," Ben groaned in a rough voice.

Audley pulled his fingers free and lined his cock up with Ben's ass. He started to push inside slowly, overwhelmed by the tight silk surrounding his cock, when Ben suddenly pushed back until Audley was balls deep inside the man. Audley froze as his entire body shuddered with what he could only describe as an electrical shock that sent pleasure pulsing through him.

"Fuck me, damn it!"

Audley grinned, pulled from his stupor by the ferocity of Ben's words. He grabbed the man's hips and began thrusting inside of him as fast as Ben had been fucking Stefan. The full moon mating thing was quickly becoming clear to him. It was a fuck fest of epic proportions, the harder and faster the better. Audley suddenly understood the need for a butt plug and lots of lube.

"Harder!" Ben shouted. Audley tried harder but he wasn't sure how much *harder* he could get. He could already feel sweat dripping down his back. His breath came in rapid huffs. No wonder Ben had two mates. He was the biggest man Audley ever met. He needed two mates just to keep up with him.

"Love you, Ben," Audley shouted as he felt his cock thicken, copious amounts of cum filling Ben as Audley's ecstasy overcame him. Audley didn't know if it was him coming in Ben's ass or his words that did the trick, but Ben suddenly cried out, his body stiffening as his inner muscles clamped down on Audley's cock.

Audley thrust a few more times, then slowly pulled away from Ben just as the man collapsed down on top of Stefan. He moved over to lie down next to his two mates, reaching over to gently brush the hair back from Stefan's flushed face. He could see that Stefan's were eyes closed as the man slept but his breathing was normal. He even had a sweet little smile on his face.

"So, that's the full moon mating, huh?" he asked as he looked at Ben.

Ben chuckled and nodded.

"When do you shift back?"

"You don't like me like this?" Ben asked.

"I think you're wonderful like this," Audley replied. He leaned over and gave Ben a quick kiss on the cheek. He wasn't sure how to kiss his small muzzle. "I just think we can only handle this about once a month. Walking upright might be an issue."

"That's why it's called the full moon mating, baby." Ben chuckled. "It only comes once a month because it takes that long for us to recover."

"I'm good with that."

"Yeah?"

Audley nodded.

"So, you're not afraid of me like this? I should shift back to normal in a little while"

Audley could hear the hesitation in Ben's voice even through the strange, rough tone it had to it. He smiled and scooted closer until he could wrap an arm over Ben's furry shoulders.

"No, you'll always be a big bad wolf, but you're my big bad wolf."

Chapter 11

"How is he?"

Ben turned from where he watched Audley and Stefan swim in the lake with Nate, Keeley, and Ethan—a few of their friends—to see Devlin standing next to him. "He's okay."

"Any lasting effects?" Devlin asked. "Stefan mentioned to Zac that Audley was having a few nightmares about killing his brother."

"He's pretty much over those, but yeah, it was kind of hairy there for a while." Ben went back to watching his mates play in the water. "I knew he suffered some terrible things at the hands of Dane and Oliver. I just didn't know how horrible until we found them in that dungeon. Dane was a sick freak."

"How long did Dane torture Audley?" Devlin asked. "Has he said? Zac knows that their father died several years ago, and according to coven law, until Audley was mated, Dane had sole control over him."

"That's such a fucking stupid law," Ben snapped. He waved a hand toward the water. "If Audley or Stefan had been allowed out on their own, Dane never would have been able to hurt them. Oliver either."

"Our laws are set in place to protect us, Ben," Prince Zacarius said as he walked up to stand beside Devlin. "Our young are not in control of themselves or their need to feed. Our laws are there to protect them while they learn control."

"But you have no one to investigate if those in charge are good people or not," Ben said. "Look what happened to Stefan and Audley."

"I agree, which is why I've set up a school and implemented a new law that states all young must be trained at the school," the prince said. "I'm searching through my coven for the best-qualified people, and I will be putting them in charge of training, with me at the head, of course."

"Seriously?" Ben asked in surprise.

"Very," Prince Zacarius said as he frowned. "Stefan and Audley ultimately fell under my leadership, and I let them down. It won't happen again. I'm just sorry that this change had to come at their expense."

"I don't know what to say," Ben said quietly. He felt like a heel for yelling at the prince, but he also ached from the pain his mates went through. "I know Stefan and Audley will both be thrilled to hear of this. It will mean a lot to them."

"I've also had several long discussions with your alpha, Daniel. We've decided that the war between our people needs to end permanently. As such, several of my new students will be werewolves, as will some of the teachers." Prince Zacarius's hand trailed down Devlin's chest. "My handsome mate has been put in charge of the werewolf program. I think he'll do beautifully teaching werewolves and vampires how to intermingle. It's always worked for me."

"You're biased," Devlin insisted as he wrapped an arm around the prince's waist and pulled him close.

"Granted, but the idea is still sound," the prince said. "Only by learning from each other can we learn to live together. And I'd say with the family and friends we have here, we are well on our way."

"We are, aren't we?" Ben looked back out at his mates. They looked to be having a blast, laughing, playing, and splashing water at each other. Ben suddenly felt the need to be closer to them.

"Would you hold this for me?" he asked as he held his soda out to Devlin. The moment Devlin took the drink, Ben whipped his shirt over his head. He glanced at Devlin and Prince Zacarius. "I have two mates to go get wet."

As Ben took off down toward the water at a full run, he heard Prince Zacarius talking to Devlin behind him. "They're in the water. Aren't they already wet?"

"There's wet," Devlin replied, chuckling, "and then there's *wet*."

Ben just made it to the edge of the water when Stefan and Audley spotted him. Audley shrieked and started swimming for all he was worth in the opposite direction, Stefan right behind him. Ben waded in up to his waist and then swam after them.

It didn't take Ben any time at all to catch up with Audley and Stefan. He grabbed one mate and then the other, pulling them both into his arms. They bounced in the water for a moment and then started to sink.

Audley shrieked again and grabbed for Ben, wrapping his arms around Ben's neck. Stefan just laughed, but he too wrapped an arm around Ben's neck. Ben now held both men in his arms as he floated in the water.

Ben backpedaled until he felt his feet touch the ground and stood up, still holding Audley and Stefan suspended in his arms. He knew with their shorter heights that if he let go of either of them, they would sink. Ben wrapped his arms under their asses and lifted them closer.

He felt their legs wrap around his waist as he leaned in to give first Audley a kiss and then Stefan. Even if he couldn't smell their instant arousal because of the water, he could feel their response in the cocks that hardened against his hips. He could see it in the twinkle in their eyes as they looked at him.

Ben grinned. "Who's afraid of the big bad wolf?"

THE END

WWW.STORMYGLENN.COM

ABOUT THE AUTHOR

Stormy believes the only thing sexier than a man in cowboy boots is two or three men in cowboy boots. She also believes in love at first sight, soul mates, true love, and happy endings.

Stormy lives in the great Northwest region of the USA, with her gorgeous husband and soul mate, six very active teenagers, two boxer-collie puppies, two old biddy cats, and three fish.

You can usually find her cuddled in bed with a book in her hand and a puppy in her lap, or on her laptop, creating the next sexy man for one of her stories. Stormy welcomes comments from readers. You can find her website at www.stormyglenn.com.

Siren Publishing, Inc.
www.SirenPublishing.com

LaVergne, TN USA
27 October 2010

202454LV00007B/128/P